I0761693

THE BURNING ORIGIN

ALSO BY

DANIELE MENCARELLI

Everything Calls for Salvation
The House of Gazes

Daniele Mencarelli

THE BURNING ORIGIN

Translated from the Italian
by Octavian MacEwen

Europa
editions

Europa Editions
27 Union Square West, Suite 302
New York NY 10003
www.europaeditions.com
info@europaeditions.com

First publication 2025 by Europa Editions

Translation by Octavian MacEwen
Original title: *Brucia l'origine*

This work has been translated with support from the Italian Ministry of Culture's Centro per il libro e la lettura.

Library of Congress Cataloging in Publication Data is available
ISBN 979-8-88966-142-9

Mencarelli, Daniele
The Burning Origin

Cover design by Ginevra Rapisardi

Cover illustration by Elisa Lipizzi/Mimaster

Prepress by Grafica Punto Print – Rome

Printed in Canada

CONTENTS

For the overwhelmed

THE BURNING ORIGIN

I
Anio Vetus Aqueduct

1

The classic mountain antipasto.

Two steel trays. On one, cured meat: ham, salami, cured pork loin, and mortadella. On the other, cheeses: chili-flavored cheese, caciotta, and pecorino.

Tania waits for her son on the edge of her chair, straining toward the front door. Giorgia watches her mother's nervous anticipation with a smile, though her accustomed eyes give nothing away.

"Mind you don't fall over, Mom. He said he'll be here in two minutes. Tell her, Dad."

Mauro shakes his head and says nothing, as usual. But it is the benign silence of someone who agrees with no objection.

Tania nods to her daughter but changes neither her position nor her expression.

Her eyes are ablaze with light, pure love.

Here is Gabriele at the door.

He is the spitting image of his mother.

He has her chestnut complexion and almond eyes. As a child, he was often mistaken for a girl on account of his soft features. This softness has remained, only tempered by the beard on his jaw.

Mother and son gaze at each other, reuniting through their eyes.

Tania clenches her fists. She wants to flail her hands around like a child consumed with joy. But she restrains herself.

Then kisses follow hugs.

2

It's been four whole years. I know there was the virus. But that's a long time."

"We did a video call every Sunday, Mom. And on top of Covid, I was swamped with work. Ever since we started again, we've been slaving away at least ten hours a day."

Gabriele snatches a slice of salami.

"Great, you got some charcuterie boards."

All the while Giorgia has been watching her brother with a wide, sincere smile. At times she is seized by melancholy, but she hides it well.

"Charcuterie boards? You've gotten so Milanese. Hear that, Dad? It's still called antipasto here. You're not in Via Monte Napoleone. You're in the Don Bosco neighborhood. At the Piccola Sardegna restaurant in Via Sofia. The place where the Bilancini family has always celebrated whenever they need to celebrate."

His sister wastes no opportunity to poke fun at her brother.

"Yeah, I'm Milanese through and through now. No kidding. I can't stand you Romans with your traffic and garbage. You're all so rude."

He rose to the challenge, responding like a stereotypical Milanese. He turns serious again:

"How's the salon?"

Giorgia swells with enthusiasm.

"I haven't become a world-famous designer, but few hairdressers can beat me. Look at Mom, cut and styled. She looks ten years younger."

Tania, placed in the spotlight, touches her hair with embarrassment.

"It's true. She's got magic hands. I feel guilty for making her work on Sundays. I get my hair done at home."

"Come on, Mom, it's nothing. There's only one person to thank here. Gabriele. Without him . . . "

"Forget it. I fund a business I believe in. Anyway, you're my sister." Gabriele sounds more Roman now.

"Hear that, Dad? He's been back home half an hour and he's already speaking like a Roman again. Tuscolano district forever."

Their father is often addressed, but he always responds with silence.

Tania watches him with a mix of patience and annoyance.

"You really are 'Mauro the Fish'. Say something."

She provokes her husband, but he is used to it and does not take it to heart. He just grins.

"You know what I always say. Ever since I first showed up, more than forty years ago, they called me 'Mauro the Fish'. I don't talk much. Only when I have something important to say. Everybody talks and nobody listens."

"You're right, Dad. And both of you forgive me, I still haven't congratulated you."

Gabriele looks at his parents and they start to feel shy.

"Thanks. You should congratulate your sister too. Don't forget she was there when we got married. I was almost six months pregnant."

Tania instinctively strokes her belly, then glances at Giorgia. They blow each other a kiss.

"How's the repair shop going, Dad?"

Gabriele holds out his hand to squeeze his father's.

"Same as ever. What with all the traffic in Rome, there are still plenty of motorcycles and scooters. There's all this hype about electric now. Let's see how long it lasts."

"Milan is flooded with them too. Let's hope the ecological transition works out."

His father looks skeptical.

"Transitions take a long time. In Italy they take centuries."

Gabriele laughs. Mauro the Fish seldom speaks, but when he does, he rarely says something forgettable. He has always been a kind of wizard, expressing himself through allegories, parables, and quips.

Gabriele's eyes linger on his father's hand.

Only a mechanic's son can understand and recognize it so quickly.

It is a matter of knowledge, observation skills.

Mauro's hands—though clean, with perfectly trimmed nails—are covered in cracks, tiny black branching lines, some more visible and others subtler, especially on his fingers.

The telltale sign of all those years of manual labor, grease, and engine oil.

It reminds Gabriele of other hands.

Those of his teacher. Mentor. And future father-in-law.

His Majesty Franco Zardi. Described years ago by *The New York Times* as "more of a Renaissance artist than a designer." Gabriele still remembers when he first saw him move those ethereal hands in the air, using gestures to create—out of nothing—his vision, an astounding idea that would convince everyone, clasping his slender fingers around his pencil, drawing as gracefully as an étoile on stage.

The scent of porcini brings him back to reality.

The first course has arrived.

3

I was expecting your girlfriend this time. I've seen her on a video call, but never in person. I'm a bit disappointed." Gabriele gives a regretful shrug.

"Camilla really wanted to come, Mom. She even cried when she realized she couldn't make it. But we have to deliver a project to an Arab the day after tomorrow. Also, she's not my girlfriend. I'm not a kid anymore. She's my partner. She might get a bit offended if you call her that."

Tania ruefully acknowledges this information as her son rushes to grab his cell phone. He has forgotten something important. He hastily types on the display:

Arrived half an hour ago. All OK.

There is an immediate tick on the other end, followed by a fast reply:

I really wanted to be there this time.
I'm sorry your dad is sick. He must be so upset
to miss his anniversary dinner.

We just did a video call with him.
Of course he's sad about it, but he's so sick
he can't get out of bed. He has a very high fever.
My mother promised him that the two of them
will go back to celebrate as soon as he gets better.
I love you, Camilla Chamomile. Speak later.

I love you too, Roman boy. Say hi to everyone.
Give your mom a big kiss from me.
Tell her I can't wait to meet her in person.

At first, he tried to be honest, to tell the truth.

Gabriele would love to at least give himself this justification.

But this is not the case. It is not true.

A chasm has opened up in his life that has suddenly distanced—to an inhuman degree—the lands of his past and present.

He is ashamed of his family, of the land that nurtured him.

In the world he now inhabits, the world of the rich, he hides it the way you hide a sin.

His origins on one side, and Milan and his high-status present on the other.

And him in the middle, berating himself for years for having so little courage, for his inability to simply be sincere, to ease his conscience for once, just once. To hear—from his own lips—who he is and where he comes from, fearlessly, openly, without worrying about being judged.

But no.

The only thing he can do is hide behind hypocrisies and silences, an endless chain of little lies that spare no one.

All he does is cultivate betrayal toward everyone.

4

The last spoonful of tiramisu.

"I'll finish digesting in Milan."

Gabriele has regained some good spirits. He checks his watch; it is past eleven.

"I'll go get the bill."

Tania fidgets in her chair, suddenly looking agitated. Her daughter is the first to notice.

"What's up with you, Mom? You've got the jitters."

She does not know what to say. Now her husband and son are giving her a quizzical look.

"No, it's just that . . . "

A smile spreads across her face.

"That's why."

She glances at the door.

A group of four has appeared.

"I can't believe it!" Giorgia cries in amazement.

"Look who Mom has brought you. Look what a surprise I've got for you."

Gabriele, who had his back to the door, turns around.

He catches his breath.

He seems to be sinking into an abyss from which it is impossible to re-emerge. He watches the newcomers almost in terror. But then some kind of giant hand lifts him up from the depths, elevating him to a childlike joy that lights up his face until it turns purple with emotion.

One of the guys in the group quickly strides over to him,

stopping within an inch of his face. His glistening eyes turn watery. He cannot be any taller than five foot two and weigh any less than a hundred and eighty pounds.

"How many years has it been?"

Gabriele tries to make a mental count of how much time has passed but stops when he realizes that many years have gone by. Too many.

"Marcello, you look identical, the same as ever."

Marcello is overflowing with childlike, innocent happiness.

Now Gabriele's eyes start to glisten too.

They tightly embrace.

"Who's this 'Marcello'? I'm Lello. For everyone and always. I'll tell you how many years it's been. Eight. You realize it's been eight years since we've seen each other?"

In the meantime, the other three have approached. The tallest guy, who has a dark complexion and a slightly crooked smile, touches Gabriele as if to test—with feigned, exaggerated delicacy—that he is actually there.

"Is that really you? Unbelievable. I can touch you, right? You've got to ask celebrities for permission. How about the woman your mother told us about, where is she? Does she know you're together?"

Gabriele laughs.

"Cristiano Pontrelli. You always were an asshole, and you still are. I grant you the right to touch me."

They exchange a swift embrace. Cristiano seems more reserved, more adult than the others, but he is also happy to see his friend again.

"Don't I get a hug, Francesco?"

Gabriele asks and his wish is granted.

Francesco gives a sad smile. He tries and fails to hide his unhappiness. He would have a handsome face if he were not crushed by a pain made even more apparent by his attempts to contain it, to not let it show.

"I'm the same as ever. I wait to be asked."

He tries to deflect with irony. Gabriele gives a grudging nod. He says nothing more.

"Hi, Vanessa."

They clutch each other awkwardly. It does not take much to figure out that they used to be involved.

"You look the same too."

Gabriele knows he is lying, and so does she.

"Not exactly the same. I wish."

Her face really does seem different somehow. It is marked by something unnatural: her swollen lips, out of proportion to the rest of her features. Gabriele tries to smile without giving his observation away, but there is no knowing if he succeeded.

Meanwhile, Marcello has pulled a carefully folded magazine page from his pocket.

The top of the page features a photo of Gabriele in a dark blue suit, striking an alluring pose. A legendary '80s Roma jersey is visible under his jacket: the one with the wolf cub designed by Piero Gratton. But he is not the only star of the photo.

He is sitting on an armchair that is more like a work of art than a piece of furniture. The square legs join in an arc under the wide, circular, simple seat. The back, by contrast, plays with shapes in a way that recalls the curves of Ionic columns rendered more geometric, severe, even austere, reworked in an unprecedented manner. New. "Classic electric," as Franco Zardi put it when he first saw the project.

"Rome is rising again. Gabriele Bilancini, with his Bilancia armchair, named among the world's top ten emerging designers."

Marcello tripped on his words a few times as he read.

He immediately brings out another page from a magazine. This one shows a beautiful girl reclining half-naked in the same chair.

"Interview with Miss Granada, the singer who changed hip hop forever."

Gabriele feels embarrassed. His friend starts to take out another page, but Cristiano intervenes.

"Come on, Lello, the restaurant has to close. I've got to go to work tomorrow. We can't stay here forever. Anyhow we know Gabriele is an important guy now. That's not why we're here." He turns serious.

"It's not just your parents' fortieth anniversary this year. Congratulations, by the way." He smiles at Tania and Mauro. "I'm turning forty myself this year. Can you believe it? Actually forty. I've never been able to afford a party, but I want to celebrate this one. And you've got to be there. Considering how much life we've spent together. Don't come up with something about furniture and designs. If you don't show up, you're a piece of shit. If you don't come, don't ever expect any of us to greet you again."

Gabriele wishes he had not heard. It is as if he has slipped into quicksand. He glances at each of them, his four old friends, all serious, in agreement, but what really rattles him is the look his family are giving him. They are staring in exactly the same way as the others.

He clasps his hands together in front of his chest.

"Honestly, Cristiano, how can I . . . I've got a deadline that . . ."

"I don't want to hear excuses. Just tell me yes or no."

Gabriele runs a hand over his face and looks at his mother.

"Then you can stay a few days at home. With us."

Tania tried her best to restrain herself, but she could not help it.

Her son understands. This time he cannot do what he usually does: find escape routes. Excuses. He reverses his opposition into a smile of acceptance.

"Okay. I'll figure something out."

"Hell yeah!"

Marcello shouts, hugging him and lifting him up for a

moment. They all clap in delight. Even Cristiano gives him a close embrace and kisses him on the cheek.

"Thanks."

Gabriele is overwhelmed by the others' joy; he too is happy now, or at least he thinks he is.

It is strange to consider how tormented he felt a few seconds earlier.

His mother comes over to hug him.

"We're finally going to spend a few days together. It's like a dream."

He nods and she seems to never want to let him go.

Here it is again. Guilt.

"Unworthy."

The judge in the middle of his chest has passed sentence.

5

Father, mother, and son are driving home.

Via Lemonia opens up before Gabriele's eyes. His Via Lemonia. On one side, the buildings lined up like soldiers; on the other, Parco degli Acquedotti, a seemingly endless grassy expanse traversed by the great aqueducts that have been supplying water to the capital since Ancient Roman times.

Here is the church of San Policarpo, where his parents married, where he and his sister received baptism and first communion, where he saw dead relatives enclosed in wood, starting with his grandparents.

This is his home and guilt—at least right now—must not be allowed to touch it.

Nothing must come between him and the places he is seeing again after all these years.

Those of his childhood, the El Dorado for every human being, or at least for the lucky ones.

The various rows of aqueducts are clearly visible under the full moon. As a boy, at sunset, he imagined them as rows of silent elephants marching back to their home, to some distant land.

A message notification brings him back to reality. It is his sister Giorgia:

Back home. Reassure Mom.
Love you bro.

He turns to his mother who had insisted on sitting in the back.

"It's Giorgia. She's home. All okay."

She acknowledges her son's words with a smile. Watching her makes you think of bicycle lights and the dynamos that power them: the more you pedal, the more they light up.

Tania is fully illuminated.

"A spot almost on the doorstep. It's a miracle."

Mauro the Fish's voice always takes people by surprise.

"Ah, your dad was in the car too?"

His wife never misses an opportunity for a dig.

Father and son exchange a quick wink.

Gabriele's room is like a deconsecrated church.

Only the bed, the altar, has remained in place. The four rope-colored walls are freshly painted, and the closet has been replaced by a basic rack, the kind you find in a clothing store with an open steel frame and hangers, all empty. The desk has gone too.

Nothing else remains of the room where he lived for his entire youth. The deconsecrated church has not only lost its furnishings, but also all the little important objects and symbols required for worship.

Gabriele is bewildered. He was not expecting this.

"We had to take off the wallpaper because it was falling apart. The desk and closet were riddled with woodworm. They recommended that rope color. Apparently, it's very trendy. Maybe it is, but it just looks gray to me. I'm sorry."

Tania stares at the floor as she speaks, mortified.

"But look."

She rushes out of the room to go and open a door to the built-in closet in the hallway. She grabs two enormous envelopes and returns to her son.

"I haven't thrown anything away. Not even a piece of paper."

Gabriele lays back on his bed. Opening the envelopes, he starts pulling out what was effectively his life, from his adolescence to his youth to his move to Milan. At least, the part of his life that deserved to be hung on the walls. Starting with his legends: while his friends had Totti or Nesta, the walls of his room featured Arne Jacobsen with his three-legged chair and Alessandro Mendini with his marvelous Proust armchair. He feels a stab of emotion as he opens and sees the next poster: Marcel Breuer and his Wassily Chair.

The second envelope—also painstakingly folded—contains the steps of his career, from the first short articles in trade magazines to the work that decreed his life's revolution: the Bilancia armchair.

Now, years later, he realizes how much he owes to the maestros he had on his walls. His armchair is a happy medium between their styles and the different cultures they represented.

With its soft contours, it seems to combine Mendini's ironic, playful style with Breuer's linear minimalism. As Ottavio Landini, the doyen of Italian design critics, wrote: "The Bilancia armchair appears to connect—without any concessions to kitsch or the familiar—the great 20th-century schools with a renewed classical, even imperial, rigor, in a way that perhaps only a Roman could achieve."

"Are you angry?"

Gabriele was lost in memories, forgetting his mother standing before him.

"Angry about what? If the furniture and wallpaper were in bad shape, what else could you do? How can I be angry with you? Look how you kept everything for me. If anything, thank you."

"Thank *you*. Always."

Tania seems suddenly revived. Gabriele keeps pulling out pieces of newspaper and other mementos. There is Miss Granada's interview in Vanity Fair, the one that Marcello had.

"I didn't keep this. I was already in Milan. Did you save it?" Gabriele asks and his mother proudly nods.

"And you really ask if I'm angry with you?"

Gabriele instinctively gets up from the bed and hugs his mother.

"I can only eternally thank you and Dad."

Tania would like to endlessly hear these words, wrapped in her son's embrace.

"I'm going to sleep. I'll just call Camilla for a second. I'm beat."

"Say hi from me."

"Hi Chamomile. Everything okay?"

"My Roman boy. Yes. You?"

"Not exactly."

"Why, what happened? You know you mustn't make me anxious."

Camilla's voice turns from humorous to serious, tense, in an instant.

"Sorry. Yeah, it's no big deal. They just gave me a surprise, a real surprise. It couldn't have been more unexpected."

"How do you mean surprise?"

"I've told you a lot about Marcello and the others, about the group I grew up with. One of my closest friends, Cristiano, is celebrating his fortieth birthday on Saturday, and they basically forced me to stay. I couldn't say no. It would've been awful."

"You're such a dummy! Why would you have said no? It's wonderful. It really is. You spent all your childhood there. Your teenage years. If you hadn't stayed, I would've made you go straight back. Actually, I can stay in a hotel. I'll come up with some excuse. I want to be there too. I don't want to miss it."

Gabriele gets out of bed in his underwear and T-shirt.

"Gabriele, are you there?"

"Yeah. I've thought about it too, Cam, but my dad is in a bad way this time. We can't get his fever down. Me and my sister found a private clinic where he's going to get a CT scan tomorrow. The doctor thinks it could be viral pneumonia. He even talked about admitting him. Of course, I'm not worried for me or you, but think of your dad . . . "

"Yeah, you're right."

Camilla does an immediate U-turn without the slightest hesitation, like a triggered mechanism.

"Now go to bed. I'll talk to you tomorrow. I love you, Camilla Chamomile."

"As soon as things settle down, I want to come to Rome too. Okay then. Good night, Roman boy. I love you too. Give your mom a kiss. She must be worried sick."

When he first saw Camilla in Zardi's showroom in downtown Milan, Gabriele thought of the ancient Egyptians who erected obelisks to symbolize the sun's rays, to give thanks to the light deity.

She looked like she was made of light.

Or rather, of gold.

Blonde, with freckles dotting her pale face.

To him, she didn't resemble a being from this world.

Gabriele goes back to bed.

It has suddenly become more uncomfortable.

The people around him do not realize that he plays with them like puppets. He just has to move them the right way, from inside.

High fever. Viral pneumonia. He told this to Camilla in full knowledge of the precise point where his words would land: on his girlfriend's almost obsessive concern for the health of the sole relative she has on the face of the earth.

Her father.

She only has him.

Her Swedish mother Kristina died in 2003 after being run over on a bicycle in Milan.

Camilla has still not really gotten over it. She suffers from anxiety. She suffered from depression. She adores her father, and he returns her adoration.

No one ever considers how lonely it is to be a puppet master.

II
Aqua Marcia Aqueduct

1

Tania experienced a kind of miracle.

Although she was not physically present, she was at her son's side throughout his journey of recognition and success.

She saw without needing to see.

She would not be able to explain it in words because that would not merely be difficult, but impossible. Like trying to hold the wind in your hand. Or to catch a star.

She only knows that it happened.

Her son never left her sight.

This is how she looks at him now, holding a cup of hot coffee while he lies in motionless sleep. She stands by the bed watching over him, enjoying him after so many years.

Only the thought of the coffee getting cold rouses her from her vision, otherwise she could remain like this until the end of time.

"Gabriele."

He opens his eyes almost instantly. He seems disoriented, struggling to focus, but only for a moment.

"Morning, Mom. Thanks."

He pulls himself up and his mother hands him the cup.

"It's been a long time since Mom brought me coffee in bed."

"Too long."

"I'll do it for you tomorrow."

She seems almost offended. "Don't be silly. For me it's a way of passing time. In the last few years, I've been waking up early, really early. That's the bad thing about getting old."

"What time do you wake up?"

"At four. Half past four."

Gabriele is concerned.

"Seriously? Is that enough sleep? What do you do at four in the morning?"

"It's enough for me. Anyway, we're in bed by nine. What am I supposed to do? Nothing. I get up, then I go back to bed. I try not to wake your father up. And I think. Thinking doesn't make any noise, thank goodness."

"What do you think about for all that time?"

"Take a guess. About you. Your sister. The past. When you were little. I imagine the future a bit. Your sister has missed her chance now, but I'd like to hold one grandchild at least."

Gabriele finishes his coffee.

His mother reaches out to take the cup, but he does not return it to her.

"I'll take it to the kitchen. Next thing you'll be washing my face like when I was a boy."

Tania lets him past and ponders for a moment. Then she turns her gaze to the bed: she cannot resist.

Two swipes and it is perfectly made.

Gabriele, still in his underwear and T-shirt, wanders around the house, exploring it after not setting foot there for so long. The apartment is spacious, the way they used to make them before the '60s. There is a large living room with a door to the kitchen, then a long hallway opening onto three bedrooms, plus a single bathroom. In the mornings he used to constantly fight with his sister. Their mother always had to intervene.

He still remembers the party his parents threw to celebrate their last mortgage payment. He was around eighteen at the time. Mauro the Fish almost got drunk. It was probably his most sociable evening. He still recalls his words.

"We're finally rid of it."

Looking around, Gabriele is reminded of how his mentor Franco Zardi reacts when he is confronted with something he does not like.

"Good things in bad taste."

When Zardi quoted Gozzano for the first time to Gabriele, he asked him if he was familiar with the poet. Gabriele nodded confidently, not knowing who he was.

The Bilancini family home is an ode to good things in bad taste.

From the modular, commercial furniture to all the junk hanging on the walls, mostly mementos of bygone days, or paintings, daubs without any worth or value.

Imagine Zardi walking—as Gabriele is doing now—step by step through that apartment. He shudders. At the mirror in the hallway he acknowledges an absolute certainty, as absolute as the rising sun: his mentor will never set foot in his home. Never.

There is a photograph in a wooden frame on the nightstand by the door; Gabriele picks it up.

Him as a child holding hands with his sister Giorgia, barely a teenager, on the Ostia shoreline.

Their parents beside them. Tania and Mauro. Young adults.

He makes a quick calculation: they were the age he is now in that picture, give or take a year.

He stares at the photo. At the faces of his family.

Nostalgia is like any other pain: it makes you suffer.

A pain without a precise location. It is not like a stomach ulcer or migraine. If anything, it is more like a kind of fever, burning, often to the point of spasm, without needing to raise your temperature.

He goes back to look at his house, the house where he grew up, the house his father bought, celebrating the last installment like a slave freeing himself from his plight.

His nostalgia does not relent, but his sense of guilt overpowers it.

A man who is ashamed of the home he grew up in.

He experiences these feelings as something obscene.

What kind of man is he?

With all the strength he can muster, he tries to clear his mind, his body, of that clutter of thoughts that no one will ever put in order. He closes his eyes, trying to calm down.

He slowly regains possession of himself, and his aesthetic taste.

The house is undoubtedly hideous, but it is his, and love is not about beautiful designs and elegance.

He forces himself to come to this trite conclusion, which solves nothing.

2

At the living room table, dressed in the same clothes he wore last night, Gabriele is absorbed in his work, his eyes glued to his laptop.

He is a different man. Concentration strains his gaze, his whole face. He has always regarded drawing as another dimension for him to travel to, a place where he has a chance to reshape reality, to embellish it, to make it look the way we want it to, for other people's happiness, for those we love.

He was still a child in elementary school when his astonished teacher Curione took Tania aside to show her Gabriele's work. She had simply given her pupils—to distract them after two intense hours of class—a homework assignment: draw your dream house.

Gabriele's classmates had obeyed as all children obey, generation after generation.

The classic square crowned by a triangle. A chimney with a wisp of smoke coming out. Countryside all around, with some trees, a few birds, and in the most creative cases a road climbing toward the mountains in the background.

But not Gabriele.

He had actually designed a house.

Not the outside, like everyone else; he had really entered inside: two long parallel horizontal lines marked the floor and ceiling, then, at regular intervals, a series of vertical lines, essentially the dividing walls, recreated the rooms.

And he had furnished all the rooms. In a rudimentary way, of course, but with an impressive, even frightening level of detail.

In particular, his teacher Curione pointed out to his mother what Gabriele—in his childlike writing—had declared to be the house's living room. Two figures, with the accompanying words "Mom and Dad," sitting on a kind of rectangle that also had a caption: "comfortable and spacious sofa where they can rest."

Tania still keeps that yellowed sheet of paper beside the gold from her children's baptisms and communions.

And Gabriele never stopped drawing.

Ironically, the design he has been working on for some time is a sofa like the one he drew in elementary school. After a chair that bears his surname—abbreviated from Bilancini to Bilancia, a more impactful name according to the marketing team—he is now grappling with his new creature.

It has been tormenting him for months in a way that closely resembles the agony of first love.

He will soon present it to Franco Zardi and then, if he approves, to the world.

The Novus sofa.

Named after one of the six aqueducts that run through Parco degli Acquedotti, the park where he grew up on Via Lemonia, in the Tuscolano neighborhood.

But something is stopping him from staying still. He is pacing back and forth, nervous, worried, at times furious.

That sofa is the summation of his life, an indelible past that seeks space in a present that is too different to understand. And his creative doubts seem to mirror his inner cracks.

He is afraid that the sofa is 'too much'.

Elegance is a matter of millimeters, grams. The smallest thing is all it takes to separate the understated from the lavish, the necessary from the superfluous. A designer, like an artist, must have the courage to mercilessly amputate.

He wants linear, simple forms that can be called 'beautiful' in time, indeed, through the ages, just like the aqueducts that filled the horizon of his childhood.

"For lunch I thought I'd do a simple starter, spaghetti with a little garlic and olive oil. Then I can do steak or chicken breast as a main course with roast potatoes on the side."

His mother's voice brings Gabriele back to the human world. He bursts out laughing.

"It's like having full board, Mom. We usually eat just one dish for lunch, a salad with some protein."

His mother has not understood. She cannot comprehend it.

"Chicken breast is fine. No potatoes, just chicken."

"Seriously? Not even roast potatoes? Why, are you on a diet?"

"No. I try to keep in shape. Anyway, we don't have much time for lunch. It's a habit. Don't worry."

She does not seem particularly convinced, let alone enthusiastic.

"Your dad is at the repair shop with his usual friends. Can you at least keep me company at the table? Or do you even work while you eat?"

He kisses her.

"Are you kidding? Of course I'll have lunch with you."

Gabriele's phone vibrates on the coffee table. He sees the name on the display and grabs it.

"Good morning, Valeria."

Gabriele signals with his index finger to ask his mother for time. She agrees, as with everything he does for that matter.

"Exactly, just as Camilla told you. Reschedule everything from Monday. Be sure to tell the Canadian ambassador. She basically stalks me. If they ask, just tell them the truth: I'm away dealing with family problems. That's fine. Of course you can call me about anything. Bye."

"Your father is superstitious; if he was here, he'd touch wood. Thankfully, we don't have any family problems."

Gabriele nods with downcast eyes. Only he knows how much falsehood his words contain every time he opens his mouth.

"Unfortunately, our work never leaves you alone unless you have an emergency. Sorry for mentioning problems."

"What are you apologizing for? I'm your mother after all, you think I don't understand? As a matter of fact, I was amazed when you were on the phone. You speak so well. Such confidence."

"Valeria is my assistant. Let's say it's easy with her."

"Why, is it harder with others?"

Grimacing, Gabriele gazes at his mother. There's so much he would like to tell her.

But he tells her nothing.

"It's a bit more complicated with other people, but I stand up for myself."

"Mommy doesn't doubt it. I'm going to make you chicken breast. With nothing on the side, what a shame!"

Tania walks away, then a thought makes her turn around; she has suddenly grown serious.

"But tonight we're having dinner like human beings. I've made you two dishes you loved as a kid. It's a surprise. I'll be upset if you don't eat them."

"Mom, in the evening I eat normally. Besides, you don't think I miss your cooking? I tell all of Milan that you're an extraordinary cook."

"Just wait to see what I've made you."

3

Sleeping beauty."

Gabriele was blissfully curled up asleep.

He finds himself facing Marcello, who wears a grin that could not be any broader.

"You're back home after eight years. You're not seriously planning to stay cooped up here all the time?"

"Hi Marcello."

His smile instantly shatters.

"Again with this 'Marcello'. I'm Lello. Is there something wrong with your memory? Have you bumped your head? Lello. Lel-lo."

"Hi Lel. Where are we off to?"

It is as if a bulb has been switched on; Marcello's smile instantly lights up again.

"Ah, right. Now let's think . . . How do you mean where are we off to? Where we always go."

Gabriele tries to reconstruct, retying threads, pieces of memories and life. The result seems to leave him rather incredulous.

"To Signor Antonio's. You still go to Signor Antonio's?"

"How do you mean 'still'? Where else would you go?"

"Is it still open? And more importantly, is he still alive?"

"Who's going to kill him? He's eighty-six years old, though he's selling up soon. I don't want to think about it. To a Chinese family. Can you believe it?"

"Do you still go there every day?"

"Not just me. We do. Our group. After work—for those

who work of course—we always go to the same meeting point."

"I'm supposed to be working. I'm sorry."

"Come on, are you really going to stay shut up at home until Saturday? You'll see the places where you grew up. Surely, you'd enjoy that?"

It was Tania who replied, entering her son's room and going over to give Marcello a hug.

"How's your mom?"

He shrugs. No one would guess he is thirty-five.

"Same as always. In bed. But she's alive and that's enough for me. Her mind is the same as ever. You know her, she's a pain in the ass, but only on the surface."

"Say hi from me."

"Sure. Well then? What have you decided, sleeping beauty, are you going to be a mummy at home or come out with me?"

"Come out with you. So how have you done it?"

Marcello does not understand and neither does Tania.

"I mean, how have you managed to stay just as you were eight years ago? The same . . . everything, the same places, same life, identical to how I remember you. How have you done it?"

It sounds like a compliment, and perhaps it is, or it is the exact opposite. The recognition of a kind of immobility that does not seem humanly possible, or rather, a reiteration of the same life without wanting anything else.

Gabriele is attracted to it and at the same time—he cannot deny—sickened by it when he thinks of everything he has accomplished in the past eight years.

"How have I done it? I eat, drink, and support Roma."

Marcello laughs and pats Gabriele on the back. Gabriele lets it go, but he would have liked to pursue it, even though he is the first to know that there is no answer to his questions. It is the way life has turned out—the way life turns out in general—that drives people or keeps them in chains.

Fate sets some on a journey, as in his case, while it crystallizes others like insects in amber, forever immobile.

"I'm so happy to see you again."

Another hug ensues.

Marcello is wearing a Gucci-branded black T-shirt one size too small. It does not take an expert to see that it is fake, a blatant knockoff. The T-shirt is paired with Adidas sweatpants and a pair of Nike high-tops. There must be a height difference of at least eight inches between them.

Gabriele walks beside his friend along Via Lemonia and all the while he watches him, studying him. They went through kindergarten, elementary, and middle school together.

When an adult looks back at their childhood, it seems like an infinite time, centuries long. Yet it is just a few years. Twelve in all, at most thirteen. Then puberty explodes, adolescence. Your senses bloom and you become something else.

"It's more like June than April. Lucky I'm in short sleeves."

"True."

"You should've seen when the head of the Lazio fans, Diabolik, was murdered. We couldn't live for two weeks. Via Lemonia was like a movie set. There were more reporters and guards than residents."

"I followed everything in the newspapers."

Gabriele replies without ever taking his eyes off him.

He thinks of his colleagues in Milan, as well as those in London, Tokyo, and New York. They have the dignified posture of those who belong to the elite, even when dressed as tramps, very rich tramps whose poverty is reconstructed with garments worth thousands of euros. Who knows what they would make of Marcello.

While nostalgia feels like a fever, at times delirious, guilt is more localized. A cramp between the mouth of the stomach and the throat, a kind of reflux, not of gastric acid, but of a guilty conscience.

The sky comes to Gabriele's rescue.

It soars celestial as far as the eye can see, looming over the entire Parco degli Acquedotti, a vast area of countryside made up of rises and falls, crops, olive groves, and even a flock of sheep. Looking at that park, you would never guess that it borders one of the most densely populated neighborhoods in the world: Appio Tuscolano. And one of the dividing lines between what was once the Roman countryside and the rampant urbanization since the postwar period is Via Lemonia itself.

There are few such open spaces in Milan.

That vastness makes Gabriele's breath race. It seems to infuse him with sudden energy, changing the complexion of his mood.

"Here's Signor Antonio's bar. Same as ever."

Marcello stretches out his arm and points a hundred yards away, beneath one of the buildings overlooking the park, to a bar with outdoor chairs and tables.

"Don't tell me you're not happy."

Gabriele nods, and it is true: the last stretch of the walk was like medicine. Seeing Parco degli Acquedotti again has reconnected him to his past.

He has gradually regained and reconstructed his bearings.

"Lello old fellow, I'm happy."

Lello stops.

"Now you remember what you used to call me!"

Gabriele keeps him in suspense for a moment, but he cannot contain himself for long:

"Lello old fellow. In foosball it was you in goal and me in attack."

Marcello joyfully raises his arms to the sky.

4

"Come on, next thing we'll be claiming that Christ died of Covid. The photo is clear as day."

Cristiano is looking at the display on his cell phone. In a grainy image, Gabriele is pictured kissing a distinguished older man. At least that is what it looks like.

"They were kissing. Him and his boss, what's his name, Zardi. I mean, I love him like a brother but we're talking about Gabriele Bilancini, Mauro the Fish's son. A guy like that goes to Milan and ends up where he did. Come on, what the fuck is that about? He was always a good-looking guy. The old man saw him and bam. Then they made up some story about him getting engaged to his daughter to cover up the relationship. Jeez. I don't even want to think about it."

Cristiano crushes his cigarette in the ashtray as he finishes speaking.

He, Vanessa, and Francesco are sitting at a table outside Signor Antonio's bar. The group from the surprise that Tania orchestrated last night at Piccola Sardegna restaurant.

"I've no doubt about it either. You don't make it unless you have connections. They give you a taste of it and then they snatch it away. Scumbags."

Francesco speaks in a barely audible voice, always distant, listless. He only glances at the photo.

"I don't want to see it. It's like the billionth time it's being shown around. It was all over social media too."

Vanessa comments on what seems to be a well-worn

discussion without taking her eyes off her phone, continuously typing, focused.

The trio have not realized that Marcello and Gabriele are approaching.

The newcomers watch them from a distance. The conversation around the table does not look particularly entertaining. And you cannot help but notice that everything they are saying to each other revolves around something contained on a phone.

"They must be talking about Francesco. He's not getting any better. They're bombarding him with drugs. We try to cheer him up, but it's no use."

In truth, Marcello is afraid that something else is being discussed at that table.

Gabriele shares the same fear. Actually, he is certain of it.

Nothing remains of the serenity evoked by the places of his youth.

He quickens his pace to reach the table.

"I'll bet a euro I can guess what you were talking about."

Gabriele remained standing as he spoke.

Vanessa puts her phone away as soon as she hears him. Cristiano notices this and gets irritated:

"Hey, you don't say a word to us, but the moment Gabriele turns up you put your phone away."

She blushes but is certainly not intimidated.

"Cristiano, you'd come second in the world ranking of assholes. You get two salaries a month at your house, yours and your wife's, but I live alone on a single salary. It's not easy. I should get alimony from my ex-husband, but he's worse off than me. I use my phone for work, if you can call it that. I resell second-hand clothes and makeup on a site that gives me a percentage. It's one or two hundred euros a month at most. But it's like gold for me. Anyway, I've told you all this plenty of times, but you're too self-centered to listen to other people."

Cristiano keeps his cool and turns back to Gabriele, who is still standing by the table.

"Stop standing there, Gabriele, you're making me anxious. And come on, let's play. Let's see if you can guess what we were talking about."

Gabriele sits down and Marcello follows suit.

"You were talking about the photo. The photo of me. The one with Zardi. You've always played the tough guy, now let's see if you have the guts to deny it."

Cristiano glances at the others. Both Francesco and Vanessa are motionless, not knowing what to do or say.

"You've won a euro. We were talking about that photo, but we weren't . . . "

"Sorry to interrupt. But on this subject, if you don't mind—since I lived it—I'm the one who can actually tell you the truth."

Cristiano has always been—or at least has always considered himself—the group's leader, partly on account of his age, given he is four or five years older than the others. He nods: let him speak.

"You guys know more than anyone how much I've always loved drawing. I've told everyone the same story of what happened. You should know it better than anyone because you were the ones I shared it with, at least at the beginning. Nine years ago, I sent the design for the armchair and other pieces to someone who was a legend to me. After a few weeks I got a phone call. 'This is Franco Zardi. Nice to meet you.' I couldn't believe it. He invited me to Milan to discuss my work. He liked it. I still remember his exact words: 'It has genuine harmony, not affectation.'"

Gabriele looks at each of his friends in turn.

"This is what you already knew. Now I'll tell you the rest. I went up to Milan and started working at Zardi's studio. A couple of weeks later, I met his daughter and instantly fell in love. After a year, just like that, Franco personally tells me that he's going to present my chair to the international market. In my name. You can't understand what that means for a young designer. Usually when you're starting out the studio you work for puts their name on your projects. They basically steal them. But not in my case. Me. Gabriele Bilancini. A guy who got his design degree in the Lazio region. The years flew by after that. The Bilancia armchair made a splash and all of a sudden I had people wanting to interview me. Then two years ago that damn photo was published. We were finishing the process of setting up our space at Milan Design Week. Franco asked me to give him a hand moving a table from his new collection. He's obsessively perfectionist. It's true, in the photo it looks like we're kissing, but it's an optical illusion. The photo flattens everything. It doesn't show that there was at least forty inches between us."

"You don't owe explanations to anyone, Gabriele. Don't dwell on it. Relax. What can I get you to drink?"

Marcello, seeing his friend with swollen veins in his neck and red eyes, has tried to stop that raging torrent, but Gabriele does not even listen to him.

"Do you know what it means to work day and night for what you've always dreamed of? Taking language classes on Saturdays and Sundays when everyone else is resting because I didn't know anything aside from Italian and Roman. Never stopping. And eventually seeing your dream come true. Then all it takes is a photo. Franco Zardi and his studio are in the top fifty most famous Italian brands in the world. Obviously, he was the one they wanted to target to create a scandal about him. Franco shook them off like dust and they assassinated me instead. It's not about homosexuality. If I'd turned gay, I'd admit it. That's not the issue. It's seeing all that hard work go up in smoke in a second. It's nothing to do with work or talent: that guy is the boss's new flame. It took me months to recover."

The four friends listened.

"I believe you, Gabriele. I was never in any doubt."

Vanessa states her thoughts, looking at him with a smile full of admiration.

"You don't even have to ask me. You've been drawing since you were a kid. You've spent your whole life drawing."

Marcello follows Vanessa without the slightest hesitation.

Francesco shares the others' thoughts; he stays silent, but you can read it in his eyes. Even Cristiano seems convinced in the end, but there is one thing he cannot swallow.

"I believe you too, Gabriele. It's just the gay thing. So, it wouldn't matter if you were a fag? That's cool with you?"

"Sure. What's the problem with that? I don't get you."

"Nothing. These days if you're not a fag it's almost like you have to be ashamed."

Gabriele's lips curl.

"Why? Do you have a problem with someone being gay?"

Cristiano laughs it off.

"No, no. Nowadays the problem is being straight."

At that very moment, a notification arrives on Gabriele's phone: a message from Camilla.

Hey, how's the reunion going? Do you miss me?

He walks off to write.

It's going okay. My friends started talking
about that photo. I'll never escape from it.

What are you talking about?
You've already escaped.
It's dead and buried.
Of course there'll always be someone
who brings it up. But everything travels

at the speed of light now.
Gab, that photo is like a billion years old.
It's meaningless now.

If you say so. I love you, Camilla Chamomile.

I love you too. Speak tonight, Roman boy.

"What can I get you?"

A graceless voice—still going strong—asks the whole table.

"Do you recognize this guy, Signor Antonio?"

Signor Antonio has a powerful frame and thinning hair. He is wearing a blue shirt that has not seen the laundry for a while. He stares at Gabriele.

"Mauro the Fish's son. The one who made it big in furniture. You had kinder eyes as a kid."

"Let's go for five spritzes. Is that okay for you, Gabriele?"

"Yeah, perfect."

Signor Antonio shows his age when he starts to move: he has a slow gait, slightly bowed to one side.

When he walks, it is as if old age is gripping his legs.

5

The spritz glasses are empty and there are many more than five.

"Of course, Gabriele, you've been the luckiest in every sense."

Cristiano is still running the show.

"Why?"

"How do you mean why? Look at Lello. He looks like a monk. He's got the perfect tonsure."

He points to the nape of Marcello's neck; it is almost completely hairless. Marcello takes offence. His hairstyle is the same as it was when he was a young boy: a crew cut, shaved clean at the sides. But signs of baldness, patches, are plain to see.

"Whatever, man, you're thinning too."

Cristiano looks at his friends around the table.

"I love winding him up about his hair."

Everyone laughs; they can all feel the effect of the spritzes.

With his distinctive gait, Signor Antonio has returned to their table with a tray.

Everyone helps him to put the glasses on it.

"When we're done, I'll come and pay. It's been a long time since I've shown up, so it's the least I can do."

"So long as someone pays, it's all the same to me."

Gabriele smiles at him.

"You're just the same as ever, Signor Antonio. You haven't changed a bit."

"It's you who change. Not this leopard."

He walks back to the bar at an even slower pace now the tray is full of glasses.

"Signor Antonio has betrayed us too. In a month we'll have Jackie Chan and family here. These days there are more Chinese bars than Roman ones."

"Yeah, I can't believe we won't see him around anymore."

Francesco, the least talkative of the group, concurs with Cristiano.

The atmosphere changes to gray, gloomy.

"At the end of the day it's normal. Time passes. Look at us. I really can't believe I'm thirty-five now. What generation are we supposed to be? Millennials, right?"

Marcello spoke in a slightly slurred voice. He does not seem to hold alcohol well.

"No. We're generation A. A for Assholes."

Already regretting her snap reply, Vanessa is looking apprehensively at Gabriele. She clearly cares about not making a bad impression.

Fortunately, he laughs, though without much conviction. He seems to have something on his mind; his eyes are locked on Cristiano.

"When you were talking earlier, why did you say 'Signor Antonio has betrayed us too'? Who else has? I'll wager another euro: want to bet I can guess?"

Cristiano seemed to be waiting for this. He straightens his back and stretches out his arms, composing himself in his chair.

"You've won another euro. If you carry on like this, I'll go broke."

"So why do you think I'm a traitor? Because I moved away for work? Because I got lucky? Aren't your mom and dad from Basilicata? Are they traitors too? It's true. I haven't shown up here for eight years. But I've told you why. Because I never stopped. If you consider me a traitor, why did you invite me to your party in the first place? Why am I here?"

Cristiano does not respond. He is not in his usual argumentative mode; he is saddened, even heartbroken.

"Gabriele, do you remember Signor Antonio's squat toilet?"

"What's that got to do with it?"

"Tell me. Do you remember it?"

"Of course I remember it."

"Who did you piss in it with the first time?"

Gabriele is struck by the memory. He looks at Cristiano, at his dark face with nothing good on it.

"With you."

"You're right, Gabriele: life decides for us. And no one can judge anyone. But we lived as brothers for years, and from one day to the next you disappeared. I suffered. All of us did. You and your mom and dad were like family. We used to eat and drink together as kids."

Cristiano knocks back his last sip of spritz.

"And there's one thing you should remember. You're smart because of this neighborhood, because of what we experienced together. Being born in certain places speeds up your brain. It's like a jungle. Rich people are slow. Do you remember when Corsetti invited us over? The guy who spent a year at our school and then ran off. What was his dad? A senator? Minister? Remember when he invited us to his birthday? I still remember the villa on the Appian Way."

Everyone goes back in time, joining together in memory.

"Do you remember how his friends were like old fogeys? Such a pain in the ass. They were so dull. At fourteen they seemed older than my granddad. How long did we last at that party?"

"The time it took for you to piss inside his perfume bottle."

Everyone bursts out laughing, even Francesco. Marcello chimed in with perfect timing.

"Let's stop dwelling on the past or I'll get depressed. There's something I've been wanting to ask you Gabriele, but I'm a bit ashamed."

He has hunched forward in his chair from embarrassment.

"You can ask me anything, Lello old fellow."

"*Anything* anything?"

"Anything you want."

"How . . . well . . . how loaded are you?"

"How do you mean?"

"It shows how many years you've spent away from Via Lemonia. He's asking you how much money you've made, how rich you've gotten."

Cristiano spells it out. Gabriele looks like this was the last question he expected. He can feel everyone's eyes on him.

"Well, obviously some jobs . . . make you money."

"I'll help you out: are you more Lamborghini or Mercedes?"

"Lamborghini, Lello old fellow? I haven't made that sort of money. It's not like I get all the profits from the chair, just a percentage. Zardi's studio pockets most of it."

"So, you're Mercedes?"

"Yeah. Mercedes, yeah."

"What series?"

"That's enough, Lello, you're obsessed with these cars."

Vanessa interrupts what was turning into a kind of interrogation. In fact, Gabriele was enjoying it.

"Money is everything. When you have money, you live; when you don't, you die."

Everyone agrees with Cristiano's words.

Gabriele nodded to please the others, but he clearly thinks otherwise.

"That's partly true."

He would like to swallow back the few words that slipped out of his mouth. His remark is met with dead silence. His friends watch him in suspense, waiting for him to continue.

"It's true that you die without money. That if you have a problem and you're broke, that problem gets a hundred times bigger. You go crazy without money. There's no denying that.

But it's cursed. I don't really know how to put it . . . It doesn't work the other way around either. When you have it, when you have a lot of it, you realize that ultimately you're still you. I mean, money doesn't give you what it promises. If you're not happy, at peace, you can't buy these things."

A gaping chasm has opened between Gabriele and the others; they stare at him as if he were an alien. None of them seem to even remotely take his words into consideration.

"I know it sounds like a load of bullshit. But it's true. I know billionaires who are miserable as hell. Because they have no more desires, nothing left to pursue. Anyway, when it comes to things that matter, there's no difference. Death and fate don't care about your bank account."

No matter how many words he lavishes on his friends, the gulf between them does not get any smaller.

"Let's not kid ourselves, Gabriele, money is everything. It fixes everything: health, beauty . . . Of course, you wind up dead whether you're rich or poor. But it's about how you get there."

Vanessa is the first to answer him.

"Money saves your ass, even when it comes to dying: if you don't have money, they'll make you die in hospital like an animal."

Francesco speaks next, his eyes turning from vacant to spirited.

Marcello says nothing, but he stands with the others.

Cristiano's expression has changed. You can see the anger coursing through him from a mile off.

"Money. We're talking about life, not death. Everything is more confusing today. Take Lello. He has an iPhone that costs over a thousand euros. But how are you paying for it, Lel?"

"I made a two hundred euro down payment, then I've got to pay thirty-nine euros a month added to the phone bill for thirty-six months."

"Everything is like that nowadays. Even online. Want to buy something you can't afford? Now you can pay in installments and get instant financing. Not to mention the people who pretend to be rich. We have the prime example right here before us, don't we Lello? What brand is the T-shirt you're wearing today?"

"This is Gucci. Don't mind me Cristiano, I've been your stooge since I was a kid. Go ahead."

"How much did you pay for that T-shirt? And how much is the real one?"

"I paid twelve euros and twenty for delivery. That's how it works when you order from China: shipping costs more than the item. The original must cost five or six hundred euros. How would I know?"

"See? It's like Monopoly. They make us pretend to buy their stuff. I told you: everything is more confusing. But when you're in dire straits, when the only guarantee you have is that there's no guarantee, and you need money to live, to survive, then that's a different story. Then you become a leper. Money makes you respectable, both in life and death. Some people even have to take out a loan to pay for a funeral."

As he spoke, Cristiano never broke eye contact with Gabriele.

"I better get home, or Mom will be worried. Who knew we'd talk about such heavy stuff."

Marcello is the first to rise from his chair, closely followed by the others. He is the most dejected; he knows he was the one—with his curiosity—who spoiled the mood that afternoon. He makes an effort to return to his usual self.

"Tell your buddy Lello something: how do you put up with living in Milan?"

"The only nice thing in Milan is the train to Rome!"

They all answered in chorus, except for Gabriele. A touch of cheerfulness is revived on everyone's faces.

"What can we say against Milan?"

Cristiano starts speaking.

"There's no fog anymore and Expo has made it even more beautiful and international. What can we say against Milan?"

He directly addresses Gabriele, who agrees with him without showing any doubt.

"That it will forever remain a valley of tears with no sun, as gray as purgatory."

Cristiano bursts into laughter. Gabriele takes it on the nose. He shakes his head with the lopsided grin of someone who has just been fooled.

"Cristiano Pontrelli. You always were an asshole, and you still are."

"I'm not an asshole. I'm just honest."

Once again, their embrace is quick and slight.

Each of them goes their own way. Gabriele looks at the time and quickens his pace.

The sky has been constantly clear and bright. It is only darkening now because night is approaching.

6

Mauro the Fish, dressed in light blue mechanic's coveralls, is sitting before the small desk in his workshop. The space is no larger than three or four hundred square feet. There is a small motorcycle lift on one side to raise the two wheels that need repairing and a workbench with all his tools on the other side. The rest of the space is overrun with scooters and motorcycles; you can barely walk through them.

Gabriele watches him engrossed in some accounts or documents. If his father only knew that his beloved son had passed him off as sick, plague-ridden, in order to hide him from the eyes of the world, his world.

"Disgrace to the earth."

A nonexistent, but nevertheless ferocious voice explodes in his brain, bending his head forward. He tries to shake it off the way dogs do with rain. He snaps out of it.

"Dad?"

He turns around with his reading glasses on his nose and smiles at his son.

"Ah, what a surprise. Shall I make you some coffee?"

Gabriele gestures no.

"It's almost dinner time."

Mauro switches his phone on and checks the time. He is somewhat taken aback.

"I can't believe it. I thought it was six or six thirty at the latest. I really am getting old. If you wait for me, I'll take off my coveralls and we can go home together."

"That's why I've come."

Mauro slips through a small door and shuts it behind him. The bathroom and changing room are inside.

Gabriele, as with every place he has reclaimed from his memory since his return, is enraptured by his father's workshop, where he grew up, often causing a bit of damage. It seemed huge when he was a kid. He would come to help out and his father would play along, asking him to pass him tools and put others away. But the moment some of his friends called him he would drop everything and run off to play.

Of course, Mauro let him go.

"Ready."

Mauro turns off the lights and reaches out to grab the handle of the roller shutter.

"Don't even try."

Gabriele orders his father, who acquiesces like a child: it is Gabriele who closes the shutter.

Mauro the Fish's workshop is located on one of the many streets and lanes leading from Via Lemonia toward Via Tuscolana. It cannot be more than three hundred yards from the Bilancini family's apartment.

Father and son walk in silence.

"Aren't you tired of the repair shop? I mean, of working?"

Gabriele's question falls on deaf ears, or at least the answer does not seem forthcoming. There is nothing new under the sun: as always, Mauro the Fish takes his time.

"Why are you asking me this?"

Gabriele only had to wait.

"Because you've been working in that place since you were fourteen. And you have every right to be tired. It's no problem if you want to quit. I'll help you and Mom out. From what I understand, mechanics don't get much of a pension."

Mauro stops and gives his son a quick, very modest caress.

"To do what exactly? To waste away at home in front of

the TV? The workshop keeps me alive. I wouldn't know what to do. I'd get old before my time. Anyway, you know I love engines. After your mother and you kids, they're the thing I've loved most in my life."

Now it is Gabriele who is slow to respond.

"You know what, Dad? You're right. But if you need . . . "

"You're already helping your sister out. We're fine. Just take care of yourself. You seem restless sometimes. Even when we used to see each other on a computer screen in video calls. Maybe I'm wrong. You've been lucky, I mean, you've been successful, but life never gets easy. Don't forget that."

He takes his son by the arm.

"I just thought of a silly example. Imagine if someone came here right now and told me: 'Carry this black sack on your shoulders, but be careful, it weighs more than fifteen stone'. Fifteen stone is a lot to lift up by yourself. It makes no difference whether it's a ton of cast iron or a ton of gold."

"So true. I've missed your stories. Your metaphors."

His father brushes it off.

"What stories and metaphors? It's just some bullshit. I try to say things in a different way, that's all. If she were still alive, your grandmother would say that there's no life without hardship. It's true. Everyone sings your praises here. They think you live in Toyland where everything is nice and easy, but Toyland doesn't exist."

Gabriele clasps his father.

"The problem is whether you feel that you belong to Toyland. Some people were born there and have lived there forever, while others arrive and never shake off the feeling of being a stranger. As if they were from another species. I'd never imagined. There are people so different from us, Dad, in every way, from how they talk to how they look, what they think, everything."

Mauro pauses to reflect on his son's words. He eventually shakes his head.

"Your Dad can't give you much help on this subject. Apart from the notary on Via Tuscolana, the one who had the big Vespa. A few shopkeepers who got rich. Ah, the Alitalia pilot married to your mother's friend who died. Apart from them, I don't have much experience of rich people. I've always been here. I guess I'm an animal that has lived my whole life in this zoo we call Via Lemonia."

Father and son laugh at the same time.

They have arrived at their building.

7

The members of the Bilancini family are sitting around the table at home. Giorgia is there too.

All of them have a very generous plate of gnocchi with tomato sauce before them.

"Mommy told you she had a surprise for you. It was your favorite dish as a kid. For the main course, I've made you breaded cutlets. Thinly sliced, just the way you used to like them. Beef, of course. Dessert, too . . . "

"Apple pie. It's my bro who has come down, for crying out loud, not the Messiah."

Giorgia preempts her mother, teasing her as usual.

Gabriele and Mauro chuckle to themselves.

Tania looks at her daughter and starts to smile too.

"First: you're jealous. Second: if you'd had children you'd understand because . . . "

She pauses, unintentionally touching a nerve.

"Sorry, Giorgia darling, Mommy didn't mean it."

But Giorgia does not seem to be particularly bothered by her mother's words.

"You don't have to apologize. It's true, I married the wrong man. He not only made me suffer, but he didn't even give me a child, not one. He loved something else and it certainly wasn't a woman. You know what he loved. The only love affair he had—and still has—was with cocaine. I found out too late."

"Bastard."

Tania cannot help but comment.

"Well, the party's over anyway. I'm told he's completely lost his mind now. He's got a load of debts with people who don't mess around. I don't even know where he lives anymore."

"He was always a wretch, but it's not his fault. He comes from a family of losers. His father and uncles were all horse gamblers. They gambled away houses and shops. Compulsive vice is something that always gets passed down. Anyway, let's change topic."

Mauro the Fish closes the subject.

"How about you? How did it go with your friends? Did you have fun?"

Tania questions her son. He tries to be as convincing as possible.

"Pretty good, yeah. They talked about the photo thing, but that was a given. Otherwise, good, yeah."

"Sweetheart, anyone with good intentions can see that the photo creates an optical illusion. There'll always be some people who—out of envy and malice—want to see what they want to see. But it's been two years now. It's water under the bridge. Like they say, time heals all wounds. That photo is long gone, but you still have your talent."

Gabriele continues to look as convinced as he can manage. His gaze turns to his sister. She's in her own world, looking unhappy, perhaps at the thought of her ex-husband.

"Do you still live here in the Quadraro neighborhood?"

She rouses herself, smiling.

"Yeah, why would I move? You've seen my apartment, right?"

Her brother nods.

"It's lovely and cozy, perfect for a single woman like me. A certain somebody, this single woman's mother, says that living in Quadraro—which is only half a mile from here as the crow flies—is too far, but the single woman tells her Mom it's just fine."

"I'm only saying that. Of course it's fine. You're half a mile away. Why wouldn't it be fine?"

Tania, suddenly in the spotlight, flounders, not knowing how to respond. In response, Giorgia picks up her phone and fiddles with it until she finds what she was looking for.

"Let me start the voice recorder. Just repeat what you said a little so I can play it to you when you complain."

Tania makes a 'screw you' gesture.

"How about you two? How's the dancing going? I still remember the teacher you had when I was a kid, Ernesto, the South American from Tor Pignattara, that international maestro of salsa and merengue."

Husband and wife look at each other with sudden nostalgia.

"It's not going, actually. Ever since Covid we've stopped. We went back a few times after the pandemic ended, but it just wasn't like before. I don't know how to put it. We'd lost our rhythm. It's partly due to age; we're not exactly spring chickens anymore."

Tania spoke on Mauro's behalf too, as is always the case. Or almost always.

"Are you kidding? You're both sixty-five! These days you're still in your prime at that age. I work with professionals who are almost eighty and are planning for the future regardless. Age is all in the mind. You're young. Don't make the mistake of living like old people."

"Gab, you don't know how many times I've told them. They're getting old before their time. They're always alone. Always at home."

"For heaven's sake, we may not be centenarians, but your body changes. I have a bad back at night. I've been working since I was fourteen. It's true that age is relative, but it depends on the kind of life you have and most of all on how hard you have to work to get by."

Mauro has almost justified himself. He looks at his wife, who goes along with his words without adding anything. For once their roles are reversed.

Gabriele, even though he is taking part in the discussion, has begun to observe and hear everything with an involuntarily external perspective.

He does not know what is happening.

He is reminded of an entomologist faced with a family of insects, devoted to studying their daily life and habits. His involvement is purely scientific, not emotional. They are and will remain insects, good or bad depending on their interaction with the lives of us human beings.

His family has turned into a bunch of cockroaches before his eyes.

He is dazed, afraid.

He was meant to spend an evening in Rome with his parents for their wedding anniversary, then leave immediately for Milan the next morning at the latest. But Cristiano's invitation forced him to stay on.

He underestimated the situation; he certainly did not think it would have such an impact on his nervous system.

He is navigating in a sea with no point of reference anymore, with a compass that has gone berserk, just like in horror or science fiction movies.

The same taste always lingers in his throat.

Of guilt.

Of more.

It feels like sacrilege.

His phone vibrates on the pillow.

Gabriele had fallen asleep. He checks the display: it is Camilla, and it is one in the morning.

"Hi, is everything okay? I didn't hear from you, so I called. You know I get worried."

"Sorry Cam, I collapsed. It was an intense day."

"Because of your dad? How did the examination go?"

"No. We're a little less stressed about that now. We'll get the result of the CT scan next week, but they told us not to worry. There are no bad signs. It's severe bronchitis. The doctor prescribed him ten days of Rocephin. He still has a high fever."

"So why are you feeling this way? Because of the sofa project?"

"No, you know work is a refuge for me. Being here has worn me out . . . I don't fit in. I didn't think that staying a few more days would feel so weird. The world has changed but everything has remained static here. I don't fit in anymore. Even with my own family. And I just agonize over my sense of guilt, over everything. Not to mention my friends. You know, the ones who think money is really the cure for everything."

"Gab, that's what ninety-nine percent of people think."

"I know. The money thing was just an example, but it's the same for everything. It's like we're no longer on the same wavelength about anything. Maybe I've gotten conceited, that's true, but so are they . . . "

"You know what I went through because of my mother's death. My therapist once told me something that has always stuck with me: 'If someone loses control, they can drown in an empty glass'. My Roman boy, you've changed. You've been through a thousand experiences that have made you what you are today. Your friends, your family, they've simply had a different life. Enjoy your parents, especially your mother. And please don't drown in an empty glass."

"Thanks, darling. As they say in Rome: I've dealt myself too many cards."

"Exactly. You know what I want to do to you when you speak in Roman dialect."

Gabriele's eyes go from weary to excited in a flash.

"Then as soon as I'm back, I'll tell you everything I've experienced, but in Roman, while you're on top of me."

Camilla laughs.

"Then hurry back."

Her voice has changed too. It is lower now, warmed by desire.

"I'll be in Milan on Sunday morning. Don't make plans until Monday afternoon."

"Deal. Get here with plenty of energy."

"Goodnight. I love you, Camilla Chamomile. Thanks."

"You're welcome. Imagine if I had to thank you for all the times you've cheered me up. Good night, my Roman love."

Gabriele puts his phone away.

Yes. Maybe it is just as his girlfriend says: he should enjoy the moment and not worry about anything else, not allow it to be ruined by bad thoughts. Easier said than done.

How can you keep bad thoughts out of your head?

III
Aqua Tepula Aqueduct

1

The exact same scene repeats.

Tania, cup in hand, looks at her son as he sleeps and wakes him with her usual tenderness, very gently touching his shoulder.

"Good morning."

Gabriele reacts with less bewilderment than he did the night before, but still wakes up rather dazed.

"Good morning, Mom. Everything okay?"

"Yes, but do you always have just coffee in the morning? How about a slice of toast with some good organic jam? It might fill you up a bit, God forbid."

"No, this is just fine. I usually have some fruit midway through the morning."

She takes this as an affront.

"Well, why didn't you say so? Your father and I don't eat fruit, but I would've gotten some for you. I'll go right away. What would you like?"

Gabriele finishes his coffee and gets out of bed.

"If you have to go out, okay, but if you're just going out to buy me fruit, don't worry about it. I'll wait for lunch like yesterday."

"No, I have to go out anyway."

"Then apples and bananas."

Tania raises the back of her hand to her forehead and shakes her head.

"Silly me, I was forgetting the most important thing."

She quickly leaves the room and returns with a duffel bag that she lays on the bed.

"Mommy didn't just keep mementos for you when we redid the room. I also saved some of your clothes. Of course you'll want to get changed today."

"It's true. I hadn't thought of that. You're such a genius."

She loves it when her son compliments her.

"I only kept the things you liked best."

Gabriele pulls out the contents of the duffle bag: these are not merely pants, T-shirts, and a couple of jackets, but pieces of his life that take him back to specific moments.

Especially one Adidas T-shirt. Black.

It was the last purchase of his former life.

He was wearing that when Franco Zardi called. How could he forget it?

Obviously, he went to Milan in a jacket and shirt, as awkward as every guy who does not usually wear these kinds of clothes.

"Thanks, Mom. A nice shower, then I'll get changed and get to work."

"I'm going to tidy up. Call if you need anything."

Tania gives her son a caress. He blocks her hand with his shoulder and holds it glued to his face for a moment to feel her warmth.

Camilla's words echo in his head: to enjoy the moment, especially his mother. To banish any bad thoughts.

He has to succeed.

Gabriele is on his laptop.

He is wearing the black Adidas T-shirt and a pair of worn-out jeans.

Motionless, he stares at his sofa design, doing nothing.

He picks up his phone and quickly types.

Hi, Camilla darling. I don't know how to improve it.
My legs are shaking but that's what happens.
I've finished the sofa. And I'm satisfied.
I'll send you everything. Don't hold back.
No mercy.

Gabriele exhales deeply, then presses send.

"Everything okay?"

Tania has been watching her son for a while. If she were not flooded with love that constantly gushes from her eyes, you might say she was spying on him. She is holding a banana and an apple.

"Great. I've finished the piece I've been working on for a long time. I created a few other pieces after the Bilancia armchair, but they were little things. This is my real second child. You can imagine how important it is. I'm staking everything on this. Camilla tells me that I shouldn't worry, that my status as a designer is no longer in question, but I don't see it that way."

"You must be tense."

"When you do certain jobs, tension is part of the deal. You can take it or leave it."

"Yes, but don't stress yourself out too much. Here, even among your friends, there's an epidemic of people who are sick. I mean, from nerves."

Gabriele looks out the window.

"I think it's the age we live in. We're all a bit sick."

He answered without looking at his mother.

Tania walks over to the table and lays down the fruit she bought for her son.

"An apple and a banana. Not too ripe, the way you like them."

Gabriele shakes his head.

"You remember everything perfectly."

Tania gloats.

"If it won't get you into trouble, can I see your new project?"

"Sure. It's a sofa. I named it Novus, after one of the aqueducts."

"There's no escaping it. The places where you're born, where you grow up, stay with you forever."

Her son has placed the laptop before her. They scroll through various images from different angles.

Tania no longer speaks; she is simply ecstatic.

"It's marvelous. It looks like it was designed by nature, not by a human."

Gabriele embraces her.

"That's a wonderful compliment. One of the nicest compliments you can give. Thanks, Mom. Really."

She breaks away from her son. Her mood quickly changes. She steps back a couple of yards. She seems to be holding something back, something burning inside her.

"Speaking of birthplaces, Mommy . . . would like to show you something. But first you have to make me a promise. That what I'm going to show you and everything that comes after will be done calmly, with a smile."

She takes her son by the arm, leading him right in front of the window. She points to one of the buildings which, like theirs, overlooks Parco degli Acquedotti; it can be no more than two hundred yards away.

"Do you remember who lived in the penthouse?"

Gabriele rummages through his memory, but he cannot recall.

"It was Mercuri. My friend, the one with the husband who worked for Alitalia. They were well off. After all, nowadays, as in the past, not everyone can afford a penthouse."

"Now that you mention it, I remember."

"She died young, poor thing, two years ago. Her husband was from the North, Pavia I think, and he moved back near his relatives. It's for sale. Their daughter told me. She still lives in this area. We talk every now and then."

Gabriele has not understood, or rather, he pretends not to have understood.

"Why are you telling me this, Mom?"

Tania stays silent; she knows her son is too smart not to have figured it out. He moves away from her. He starts walking around the lounge.

"You're asking me something . . . Impossible . . . I work in Milan now. I live in Milan. I couldn't, even if I wanted to . . . "

"I don't want an immediate answer. And you promised to keep smiling. I've shown you. That's what I wanted. I'm not stupid. I'm not asking you to come back here permanently, just to make . . . this investment. It's always bad to talk about money, but right now it's really a bargain. And you could come back whenever you want, for a week now and then. You've always asked me if you could do anything for us financially and we've always told you to take care of yourself. You help your sister with the salon and that's already a lot."

A message notification interrupts the discussion. Gabriele unlocks his phone and reads. His face lights up and he closes his eyes in excitement.

"It must be good news."

Tania witnessed her son's reaction; he nods, so happy that he cannot stand still.

"It's Camilla. She saw the new design. I'll read you what she wrote to me: 'My Roman boy', that's what she calls me, 'I was moved by your Novus sofa. I love you for who you are and I adore you as a designer. It's simply wonderful. If you'll allow me, I'll pass everything on to Dad. He'll be enthusiastic as well, I've no doubt about that."

Tania goes over to Gabriele and hugs him. Each of her son's victories is her own too.

"Mommy has always had total faith in your talent."

Gabriele breaks away from his mother.

"I confirmed that she can hand the project over to her dad."

He quickly types on the display, then turns to Tania.

"We'll drink a toast tonight. I'll get a bottle of champagne."

"Mommy has cooked you another surprise. I'm so pleased. But don't forget what I told you."

He seems to have already forgotten. His mother indicates the penthouse she showed him with a nod.

Another notification interrupts them again.

"It must be her wanting to tell me something."

Gabriele gradually darkens as he reads.

"It's not Camilla."

Tania states this without any doubt; she can read her son like an open book.

"No. It's Lello. He's inviting me to his house for lunch. He says his mother wants to see me."

"Few families have had such bad luck as them."

"I honestly didn't think his mom was still alive."

"She's been bedridden for almost ten years. Tina is a woman with a heart of gold. I go and visit her now and then but less and less. I feel so guilty about it."

She takes her son's hands.

"Gabriele, even if you don't feel like it, if it's not easy, go and see them. You were like a son to Tina."

Gabriele knows this is true, but he also knows it will be laborious.

"Okay."

2

Just last summer we redid the living room."

Marcello lives in a building that overlooks Via Lucio Sestio, a boundary line somewhat similar to how Via Lemonia borders Parco degli Acquedotti. Here, however, the other side is not countryside and public parkland, but one of the most famous, historic areas of the Tuscolano neighborhood: the Quadraro.

The small living room has a wall unit on one side with a fifty-inch screen in the center and an L-shaped sofa on the other.

"I don't watch much television. I play Playstation. I only watch Roma when they play away because I've always had a season ticket for the home games. I'm a die-hard Roma fan."

"Lello old fellow, of course I remember. You're the one who has forgotten that I'm a Roma fan too."

"Whatever, you're a supporter, being a fan means something else. Anyway, who else would you support? Come on, Mom is waiting for you."

Illness is like a huge cyclone. Some people are barely touched by it: just a little wind and rain. Others live where the cyclone is at the height of its fury.

In the case of Marcello's mother, this is the motionless fury of a woman paralyzed in her bed, weighing at least fifteen stone, with nasal tubes connecting her to an oxygen tank.

The moment he sees Tina, Gabriele has the sensation that her body has become the same shape as the bed, enlarged and elongated.

Her face is the only part that has retained its original shape, although it has considerably aged. She has the complexion—Gabriele thinks sorrowfully—of the living on the brink of death.

"Come here. Let me give you a hug."

Tina embraces Gabriele, holding him close for a long time, then takes his face in her hands.

"You've grown into a man. So handsome. You always were handsome. My Lello is an angel, but he's like his father was: a potato."

Marcello was arranging the wall of medicines neatly placed on top of the bedroom dresser. He abruptly turns around, somewhere between serious and ironic:

"Thanks, Mom. Every time I leave this room I really feel on top of the world. Thank you as always."

She beckons him with a nod and as soon as her son approaches, his mother impetuously pulls him close to her, grasping him with all the strength she still has in her body.

"But you're my love. You're not a son, you're an angel. Mommy's sweetheart."

Marcello lets himself be cradled with the expression of someone who has nothing else to demand from the universe.

The little boy he met in kindergarten appears before Gabriele's eyes. The one who used to pee himself and then burst into tears. The one who constantly fell over while playing.

Who knows, perhaps life lies in these cracks of light.

When the fragility of childhood shamelessly comes back to life.

This is what Gabriele thinks.

Mother and son break apart.

"How about a little lunch and some PlayStation?"

"Okay."

"Then I'll go heat up the oven. Unfortunately, I haven't been shopping. We'll have to make do with breaded fritters and frozen sandwiches. I've got some with spinach too if you want."

"No problem. I'll eat what you eat."

Marcello walks out with his friend, casting one last glance at Tina.

"We'll say goodbye later."

She nods, suddenly looking very tired.

"I got too excited," she tells Gabriele, as if to apologize.

There are two dirty plastic plates on the coffee table next to the sofa, along with two plastic cups and a half-filled Coke bottle.

Marcello and Gabriele are playing PlayStation.

"You always sucked, but now you're a whole new level of bad."

"Lello old fellow, I haven't played since I left here. That's over eight years."

"Then maybe I should dig out some old games like an old 'Fifa'. I've got some classics too: 'SuperMario' and 'Assassin's Creed'."

"No, forget it. I've lost my touch anyway. It's better if you play and I watch."

"Maybe, yeah. I'm sorry, but you've even lost the basics. I'll look for someone to challenge online. Here he is. Now I'll destroy him."

The game in question simulates military combat in a war zone with extraordinary graphics and effects. Gabriele watches Marcello in action, cheering him on; his friend is outstanding, beating the opponent he found online in no time.

"Lello old fellow, you're a beast. If there were PlayStation Olympics, you'd be competing for a medal."

He chuckles, all puffed up.

"I'm actually one of the best in the world at this game."

"I can imagine. So, tell me . . . "

Gabriele stalls. He was about to ask him if has a woman in his life, a relationship, but he realizes this is unwise.

"Nothing . . . I wanted to know what the others are doing. I mean for work, in life."

Meanwhile, Marcello has found another player to challenge online.

"Cristiano works for a cooperative at Ciampino airport. His wife is a janitor at a school on Via Prenestina. Vanessa is a cashier at Lidl behind Giulio Agricola metro station; she separated last year. Francesco does nothing except suffer from depression."

"You?"

"Me?"

Marcello has never taken his eyes off the screen.

"I've got Mom's pension."

A message notification appears on Marcello's smartphone; it has a cover with the Capitoline Wolf and the yellow and red Roma colors.

"You should thank my phone; I would've demolished you in three minutes."

He talks to his online challenger, then leaves the game to go and see who wrote to him.

"It's Cristiano. He finished work early and is asking if we want to go to the playing field and kick a ball around."

Gabriele smiles.

"You're up for it. Great. I want to play too. I'll tell him yes. We'll get there in half an hour."

Marcello misunderstood. Gabriele only smiled because of the tremendous feeling of déjà vu that just ran through his mind.

"I'm in jeans. How can I play?"

"It's not exactly a Serie A game. We play for fun. Let's go say bye to Mom."

Gabriele obeys everything his friend suggests.

This day is devoted to him.

But his high spirits, his acceptance of everything with no complaints, stems from something else. From his sofa design that sent Camilla into a frenzy of joy.

Who knows, maybe right now, at this very moment, his boss is looking at it. He awaits Zardi's judgment as if it were a pronouncement from God.

"Mom?"

Tina had fallen asleep. She slowly wakes up.

"We're going out. Gabriele wants to say goodbye."

He approaches her and gives her a kiss on the cheek.

"Hi, Tina. You're in good hands. Lello is one of a kind."

She gives a faint smile.

"I know. Give your mom a kiss from me. She's been a great friend. As for you, I don't think we'll see each other again. Good luck with everything. You've been like a son to me."

Gabriele backs away. He tries to fight them, but his tears prevail.

"Don't say that, Mom. Remember what Dad used to tell you: there's always time to die."

"And then he died first. But forget about that now. Go and play."

"Give me a call if you need anything."

Tina answers her son with an affectionate squint.

3

The playing field is a huge level area inside Parco degli Acquedotti. The rudimentary goals are made with wooden poles planted in the ground with a shoddily nailed crossbar.

"Alright then, let's start."

Cristiano has just finished talking to a teenager in a Roma jersey who looks no older than fourteen. He is not aware of it, but when he turns his back to go back to Gabriele and the others, the young boy smiles at a thought and says something to his teammates of the same age: they all burst into peals of laughter.

"Those kids are laughing, Cristiano. I think they're making fun of us."

He turns to look at them, instantly scowling.

"Because they see us as old fogies. But they won't be laughing for long."

"Guys, I'm in jeans and I haven't played in ages, so I can't promise anything."

Gabriele is worried and at the same time eager to play; it has been so long.

"The last time I weighed myself I was one hundred and ninety pounds. And I'm five foot three. But I'm with Cristiano: let's crush them. Like when we were kids: eye of the tiger. Besides, we have the all time greatest talent of Via Lemonia with us, Francesco Abate."

Marcello is convinced.

He is all fired up.

Francesco tries to smile.

He really tries.

"You kick off. You're old so we'll give you an advantage.

The kids keep mocking them.

The game begins.

Marcello taps the ball toward Gabriele. It seems to burn him between his feet; as soon as he manages to tame it, he immediately passes it to Cristiano, who volleys it to Francesco.

He stops it, observes it, and does not seem to know what to do with it.

All of a sudden, a kind of electric current passes through that sorrowful face, that hunched body. He abruptly switches on, like a dead man miraculously returning to life, like Lazarus resurrected.

The kids become skittles as he twirls the ball between his feet.

He not only possesses technique and speed; Francesco is an ode to elegance. With his posture, his head held high, he looks like a prince playing soccer.

Gabriele is reminded of a beautiful memory.

He had only recently gotten to know Zardi. His boss called him to show him something on his computer: an old black-and-white video a few minutes long. Pablo Picasso drawing bulls. With only a few gestures, often just one, out of nowhere he created forms that quivered with intensity.

"There is no more effective definition of talent than this," Franco told him, as he watched enraptured.

Gabriele thinks the same thing now, observing Francesco in action.

It is as if exercising his talent makes him beautiful. He and everything around him light up with a wondrous light.

He skips past the last defender and then stops in front of the goalkeeper, the smallest and roundest of the boys. With a simple body feint he throws him off balance and the boy falls on his ass. Then with the sole of his shoe Francesco pushes the ball through the posts.

Goal.

Gabriele, Marcello, and Cristiano rejoice. They are not only cheering for the goal, but for that real smile, that moment of newfound happiness that Francesco is now experiencing.

They all run over to him, hugging him. He gasps for breath.

As he clutches the others, Gabriele sinks into the absence of something he cannot name. Friendship. Or brotherhood. Or full, sincere communion. Joy shared without a trace of falseness. The kind of joy that is filling him right now.

Perhaps achieving his dream was his greatest curse.

Yes.

He should have stayed with his friends who are now holding him tight. At the same level as them. Fuck the design world and the Bilancia armchair.

Camilla's smile makes him reconsider certain thoughts.

They barely have time to enjoy all the jubilation.

Francesco is like a candle burning with its last flame.

He flickers out.

That black light that imbues him with darkness returns to seize him. He doubles over. His face has turned livid.

"I don't feel good."

He goes to hide behind a tree to throw up. Gabriele and the others rush over to him.

"We've shown you the greatest talent of Via Lemonia!"

As he runs, Marcello shouts to the kids, who have been standing frozen the whole time.

First incredulous, now fearful.

4

I was there. You can't understand. I was inside San Siro with all three seating levels full. Francesco Abate, from the youth league to my first call-up to Serie A. I still have the newspaper clipping. I was doing regular training with the first team. I'd made it. Agents were after me. At night we used to go out in Milan and all the doors would open. I was the best. It's not fair. Bastards."

At a small table at Signor Antonio's, again with his eyes plunged into emptiness, Francesco is venting as he drinks some hot tea. His friends are listening to him in silence. Gabriele is the most engaged and curious; the others know that story all too well, though they are still affected by it.

"I remember when you debuted in the first team. Also, the news that Milan had sold you to Cosenza. I was still living here at home. I thought you'd continued playing. What happened?"

Gabriele asks the question.

"I played for Cosenza for seven months. I couldn't believe I'd gone from Serie A to Serie C. I wasn't training with the right mindset anymore. I wound up living a few years in Calabria. I had a woman there, but it ended badly. Then depression came knocking. The only thing that keeps me company now. Aside from these guys. Without Lello and Cristiano, maybe I would've already . . . "

"Already nothing! Give us a fucking break, Francesco! All of us here are flying blind, but always remember, those who retreat from the ditches . . . "

"Are sons of bitches!"

Everyone responds in chorus.

"The thing that I can't forget, that torments me, is that they sent me away from Milan because they resented me. Because there were guys who had a pedigree, like dogs: sons of players and managers. Soccer is like any other job. There are always people who don't have to put in as much work just because they were born in the right place."

Francesco shakes with rage until he trembles all over, his drained face twitching, his eyes narrowed, his jaw clenched.

"I've been the luckiest with design. I know that's what you all think. And it's true. But I want to tell you something. Don't think . . . I've achieved the goals we dreamed of as kids and it's not what I imagined. In the end, it all seems like a war between ants to me. They make us want so many things. They present us with so many lives as models, but then what? What really matters is feeling good about ourselves, or at least not at war. I'm one of the top ten junior designers in the world, but what good is that? It's like yesterday's conversation about money. You think that when you achieve success your life automatically changes, that you become happy and that's it. But it doesn't work like that."

Gabriele, despite his childish cowardice and all the falsehoods, could not stay silent.

"If success and money don't matter, then what are we living for? What the fuck are we doing in this world?"

Francesco looks at him, trembling. He is still shaken by rage, now rekindled.

"Ever since you arrived you've been saying that money is useless, that success doesn't change your life. Do you want to know what I really think? Those are just fairy tales. That's not reality. If you come from the bottom, if you have a background like ours, they force you out. You'll never be part of that world. They treat you like toilet paper. You can only stay in some jobs if you give up your ass and soul."

Gabriele did not expect this reaction. Whether intentionally or not, the photo that ruined the last years of his life is hovering over his head again.

"Sure, some people are willing to give up everything to be accepted, even to become their boss's lover, right?"

Francesco stares at him without answering, but that is exactly what he thinks.

"I've only told you my personal experience. Nothing more and nothing less. Some people assume that because they've failed, everyone else has to fail, and when others are successful it's only because they're willing to play dirty. I was simply telling you that all that glitters is not gold. You don't realize that you have many things that are mirages for other people, like your friendship, a neighborhood that is your home. You can't imagine the loneliness experienced in some lives. Highly successful, but cold as ice, like an operating table. Anyway, think what you like. I don't need to convince anyone."

"I was the best. And I didn't make it because they didn't let me make it, because I'm a nobody. I was the best."

Francesco is no longer speaking to Gabriele. He is no longer speaking to anyone. He repeats these words to the gentle breeze coming from the park.

Now he just arouses pity. Nothing more. A still-young guy living disguised as a dying old man, with nothing left to expect from life.

"We all seem to be depressed here."

Marcello speaks.

"Maybe. Or maybe it's life . . . the way it is. I don't know."

Gabriele does not know exactly how to answer him. He is drained by the discussion, drained by the suffering that is now devouring Francesco.

Guilt always easily conquers him.

"You can safely say that we're all depressed here. Francesco, well, he's always been. But me too. Vanessa. We're all that way here."

"Speak for yourselves."

Cristiano had been silent for too long.

"You've done a lot of talking. I don't know if you know, Gabriele, but I work at Ciampino, at the airport. I'm one of the guys who carries luggage and loses it along the way. Want to know if I'm happy? Let me tell you: I can't afford to ask that question. I have to make do with what I have, because if I try to say something, they'll all answer me the same way: I can't complain."

He lights yet another cigarette.

"Ever since you got here, you've been telling us there's more to life than success and money, but as you may have guessed, no one believes you. But one thing is true, I'll grant you that. I don't want to talk about happiness—I'd like to know who the fuck has ever actually experienced it—but I'm a man who has the good fortune to be in love. With this place, with my lifelong friends, with my wife. I envy no one, and no one has given me anything. Whatever little I have I've built for myself. I can stare Jesus Christ in the eye, and you can be sure I wouldn't be the first one to look down."

Gabriele, as if he had to pay a punishment, has just heard the exact reverse of his life. Everything he is unable to be. He is tired, offended, not with Cristiano, but with himself.

"How come we always end up talking about these things? Death. And Jesus Christ. I'll give you a good laugh now. After all, I've got to go home to Mom soon and if I get there feeling down then it's game over."

Marcello's suggestion breaks the enormous tension that has flared up around the coffee table, although the task—making the millstones that have surfaced disappear—seems somewhat arduous. He knows that he has a tough challenge before him.

"Well, then. You know the social security office in Cinecittà? By the way, if I had a plane and knew how to fly it, I'd raze it to the ground."

"You'd need some bombs too then."

Cristiano points this out just to distract him, complicating his task by teasing him. Marcello glares at him, raising his hand to make him stop.

"I know what you're up to. Don't be a jerk, trying to make me lose my thread. Anyway, I went to that office for Mom to renew a document. The usual paperwork. So, I go in and get a ticket. I had thirty-six people in front of me. After maybe an hour, I have to piss. I find the bathroom and go in. Even the social security office has been modernized: even they've got a light with a photocell. I enter, lock the door, the light turns on and I start. Suddenly it goes out. Fucking hell. I raise an arm to turn it back on, but no luck. I raise both arms. Nothing doing. Finally, even though the doctors say it's bad for you, I force myself to stop pissing. I start dancing around like a moron and the light comes back on. I finally start again. After maximum three seconds, it goes off again. So, I say fuck social security, queues and photocells, and piss in the dark from memory."

"Come on, get to the point."

Marcello gives Cristiano a look of pure loathing. The mood around the table has already lightened; everyone snickers, not so much at the story but at the way the two of them are goading each other.

"Hold it! You shouldn't have been called 'Cristiano'. You're more satanic than Christian. Anyway, I come out of the bathroom and find myself facing a little old lady with a pair of glasses twenty inches thick. Like bulletproof glass. She's shorter than me."

"Impossible."

Marcello makes an inhuman effort to ignore yet another jab, naturally from Cristiano again.

"She looks me up and down, from my shoes all the way up my pants. 'You've pissed yourself, kid'. I take a look at myself.

So embarrassing. It was true. Everyone in the waiting room was staring at me."

"So, what did you do?"

This time it is Gabriele who urges him on, struggling to hold back his laughter. He looks at his friend's round face, which has turned crimson again at the memory.

"I told the old woman: 'First, madam, I'm not a kid. I'm thirty-five years old but I'll take that as a compliment. Second, it's tap water.' I think to myself: I've gotten away with it. Instead, I hear an old hag behind me saying: 'Tap water? But the bathroom doesn't have a sink.'"

Everyone bursts out laughing. Marcello is happy with the result and at the same time mortified from embarrassment.

"So, what did you do?"

"What did I do? I left. Almost running."

More laughter.

"What did I miss?"

In a pair of skin-tight jeans, perfectly made up, Vanessa has arrived at their table. She pulls up a chair and joins them.

"Nothing. Lello pissed himself at the social security office. Nothing out of the ordinary."

Cristiano closes the conversation in his distinctive manner.

They are interrupted by a ringing phone.

It is Gabriele's; Franco Zardi's name appears on the display.

"Excuse me for a moment."

He moves at least fifty yards away.

"Hi, Franco."

"Hi Gab, how's it going?"

"Fine. I hadn't been back for a long time and my family and friends were complaining. But fine."

Gabriele's voice is crystal clear. He tries to adopt a more adult, measured tone. It is equally clear that it takes him a lot of effort to assume such an unnatural manner.

"I don't want to keep you, so I'll get straight to the point. Few people have surprised me twice; you've succeeded. Your sofa, the Novus, is remarkable, truly, and you're very talented. It reminds me of a starker version of Gaetano Pesce's 'Cannaregio' design. That was a modular project with independent units. You have given those alternating soft contours a kind of geometry that is—I don't know how to put it—emotive. Wonderful. I never told you what some of your senior colleagues said to me when I decided to take you on at the studio: 'Do you really want to hire that Roman kid? Without a single finished project? With a piece of toilet paper for a degree?' And you know what I replied? I've told you this many times: 'We have to go back to the value of the workshop, of the master and the student. All these schools merely institutionalize the gaze and taste.' But I don't want to take any more of your time. Send my regards to your family. Tell them that sooner or later they must come to stay with me in Milan, or we'll come to Rome."

"Of course. I'm overjoyed that you like the project."

"You deserve to be."

Gabriele is, as usual, torn in half. He is so delighted that his child has had such a positive reception that he clenches his fists in joy. He has been waiting for this moment for months. Yet at the same time he is terrified at the idea of the two families united under one roof.

He goes back to the table.

"Who called you? The pope? You were pulling a face like a priest when you ran off."

"It was Franco Zardi, my boss. He saw the new project and he told me that . . . "

"Ah! The one who bent you over. Everything okay, is it? He hasn't found a new guy?"

"Lello is right. You should've been called 'Satanico' not Cristiano."

Gabriele answered him in the same tone, but he did not take offense. Cristiano laughs. He is endlessly provocative toward everything and everyone; he has always been like this, ever since he was a little boy. He pulls a contrite face, or at least attempts to.

"Whatever. To make up for it, how about a round of spritz for everyone? Except for Francesco who hasn't been well. Lello is paying."

"I knew that was coming."

5

On Sunday morning I'll have to roll to Milan."

Gabriele comments on the dish that his mother has placed under his nose. There is always some truth hidden in jokes and this applies to everyone. For Gabriele, they are the ultimate expression of sincerity. Three of them are sitting around the table; Giorgia is absent.

"Your sister says hi. She had plans this evening that she couldn't change. Mommy has made you white lasagna with cream, mushrooms and ham."

"Shall we play bingo later?"

Gabriele chuckles at his father's suggestion.

"Let's hear it then. Why should we play bingo?"

"No reason. It just seems a lot like, well, a Christmas dish."

"I got a bottle of champagne to celebrate the sofa that they liked. If you want, I'll go buy a panettone too."

Gabriele indulges his father and Tania plays along.

"You used to be crazy about white lasagna as a kid." Besides, in Milan you eat—you told me the other day—'a salad with some protein'. What's that exactly, a medicine? I'm restoring your strength."

"Sure, Mom. Everyone knows that food and life are miserable in Milan."

Gabriele parries back.

"How did it go today?"

"Well. Tina says hi. I don't think she has much time left. I felt so sorry for her."

His mother and father greet the news with such similar expressions that they look more like siblings than spouses.

"Then . . . "

Gabriele pauses and bursts out laughing, leaving his parents puzzled.

"Then—you won't believe this—we organized a game on the playing field, but it barely lasted two minutes because Francesco got sick. Actually, we ended up arguing. But obviously that's not what I'm laughing about. It's Lello. He told us about one of his misadventures. I haven't laughed like that in years."

Tania is over the moon.

"I told you you'd enjoy seeing your friends again. You spent a lifetime with them, the best years."

Gabriele is not listening to his mother. The words he uttered are still ringing in his ears. Spoken without thinking, they slipped out naturally with no calculation or fear. He spoke about it just as he had experienced it.

He had not laughed like that in years.

Perhaps like never before.

Or rather, perhaps like only before.

Tania has gone from rejoicing over the news that her son gave her to a sudden thought; it is running through her mind, through her eyes, like a needle from temple to temple.

"It's already Friday tomorrow."

It is as if she has announced that some relative has passed away.

Her husband and son do not speak; they do not know what to say.

"Mom, I promise I'll come back more often. But now let's just sit down and eat. I promise you, though."

She obeys.

Even though she does not seem to have much of an appetite.

"Hello?"

"Hi. I've missed you. I know Dad called you. I imagine you must've leapt with joy."

"Yeah, he really liked the Novus. He phoned me while I was crying with laughter at one of Lello's stories. That guy is a real one-off."

"Fuck, Gab. The things you tell me make it sound like you're on vacation. Like you're camping in your twenties, always with friends, games. It's utter boredom here. Maybe I'll go for a drink with Lucia and her boyfriend tonight. That's it."

"Milan is another level. But here, now that you mention it, it's true that people are still closer. I don't know how to put it. They've stuck together over the years. The bad part is that they live the same old life forever. It would drive me crazy. This morning my mom showed me a vacant penthouse near our house. See what I mean? Even she still wants me to be closer."

Camilla falls silent. Her breathing is audible.

"And what did you tell her?"

"The truth. My life is in Milan. I felt sorry for her. She wanted to show it to me, but I . . . "

"Well, why not?"

Gabriele, sitting cross-legged on the bed in his underwear and T-shirt, runs a hand over his face, starting to break into a cold sweat.

"How do you mean why not? Do you want to move to Rome? Are you thinking straight, Cam?"

"You're so categorical. 'Move'. It's a wonderful idea. We can spend a few weeks a year there. I need to get away from Milan. I need new faces, different people. I feel caged, even with my father. Besides, your mom is right: she wants you close. Yours is alive and you can still enjoy her. And she can enjoy you, us."

He gets out of bed and starts pacing back and forth. One hand holds the phone to his ear; the other is spread open across his forehead. He curses himself for bringing up the penthouse.

At the same time, for the first time since he has been living with a chasm in his breast, he sees and feels a possible solution.

"I have to think about it, Cam. Here, I don't know how to tell you, but the life you lead, that we lead in Milan, is different here. I'm also, how can I say, a little different. I don't know how to explain it."

"Different how? Are you straight in Milan and gay in Rome?"

Camilla laughs at her joke. Gabriele also attempts to but fails.

"No. It's just that . . . I loosen up here. I don't know if you understand what I mean."

"How do you mean 'loosen up'?"

Gabriele gets back on the bed, but it suddenly feels covered in nails. He instantly springs up and returns to his increasingly hysterical circling.

"I mean that with you, in Milan, I try . . . try to be more . . . precise, presentable. With all of you I can't be what I am here, what everyone is here. You all have no idea. They're different worlds. Imagine you go to your dad and greet him with 'Alright, Franco dude, all good?'. You get it. And I'm not just talking about the way we speak in Rome. I'm talking about everything. Do you get it?"

Camilla stays mute.

This time, however, she does not seem willing to break the silence.

"Are you there?"

"Yes."

"Then why don't you speak?"

"Firstly: 'you all'. Who do you mean 'you all'? Me. Me, Camilla. That aside, I thought I was with a guy who presents himself the way he genuinely is. But no. So, tell me: which one are you really? The guy from Rome or the guy who shares a house with me? Who says he loves me?"

Camilla's voice cracks.

"I thought . . . I wish you were just yourself."

Gabriele vents the anger building up in his veins on one of the hangers on the clothes rack. He grabs it and crushes it until he hears the sound of cracking plastic.

"Camilla. Let's not overreact. And let's stay calm. I've told you this a million times. You come from one world. I'm from another. But it's one thing to hear it in a story and another to live it. I don't think you could relate to it."

"You should let me decide that. You're basically telling me that with me you're ashamed of your past life?"

"Yeah. Maybe that's true, at least partly."

Silence can become one of the most violent forms of psychological torture.

"Please don't act like this, Cam. It's like you're putting everything I say under a microscope. You're making me feel bad."

"I'm feeling bad too right now, if you must know. You said maybe that's true, at least partly. And what exactly is the other part? Maybe the fact that I'm rich and middle-class? No, worse, some kind of fucking aristocrat who puts the world in a pyramid with us at the top and the less fortunate at the bottom. You're afraid I'm going to judge your family and your neighborhood, and you want to protect them from me. That's what you think."

Gabriele wrings his hands. His whole body is vibrating, shaken by the nervousness that is now literally consuming him.

"Aren't you going to answer?"

Now Camilla is the one pressing, and he is the one holed up in silence.

"In all of this the only one discriminating against everyone is you."

"I only know that I love you, Cam. That my life has changed ever since I saw you. It's true, you're right, these days at home have reopened unfinished business. But I want you to be understanding about one thing. You've always lived in the same environment. It's not about being rich or poor. I've gone from one world to another and it's not easy. I still can't reconcile everything. That's the truth. Please believe me."

"We immediately fell in love precisely because we were different. I always thought that was something special for us: each of us found what we had never experienced in the other. Now I learn that it wasn't like that for you. That you've always seen that difference as a kind of sword hanging over your head. Good night."

Gabriele stares at the now silent phone and throws it on the bed.

He stands still in the middle of the room.

A shiver of cold. Of utter loneliness.

IV
Aqua Iulia Aqueduct

1

She was not expecting this.

When Tania entered the room with a cup of coffee, she envisioned finding her son still slumbering, like on the other mornings. Instead, she finds him at the window, gazing out at the park. At that time of morning, it is half-deserted except for a few people walking their dogs on leashes.

"Ah, you're already awake. Good morning."

Gabriele turns around and his mother's high spirits vanish.

"What's the matter?"

"Nothing. Why? I just woke up early."

"Yeah, and I'm Queen Elizabeth. God rest her soul. You know it's hard to lie to your mom. I can see how you're doing just by looking at you."

"I had an argument with Camilla. We'll work it out. I just feel bad about it."

"Why's that?"

Gabriele goes over to his mother and takes the coffee cup out of her hands. He quickly gulps it down and returns it to her.

He gives a faint smile.

"The usual relationship stuff. A little jealousy. We'll work it out."

"Of course. The world has changed. I'm sixty-five years old. I'm not an old-timer. But they used to say: 'choose wives and oxen from your own town'. Anyway, that's old-fashioned now."

"Yeah, Mom, that's really old-fashioned."

She is good at not giving it away, but she feels hurt by her son's dry, nervous response.

"I'll leave you alone. Let me know if you need anything . . . "

"Sure . . . "

"Ah, I just wanted to show you a photo. I found it in one of those drawers you forget about for years."

Tania pulls it out from the pocket of the sweatpants she wears around the house.

"Let's see if you remember it."

She puts a photograph before her son's eyes; it shows two children in costume for a Carnival party. The little girl, who is older, wears a princess dress, while the younger boy is dressed as some kind of knight from a cartoon.

The last thing Gabriele needed right now was nostalgia.

"Of course I remember. Carnival in '94 or '95. Giorgia was a beautiful child."

"So, she's ugly now? If she heard that, she'd hit you like when you were kids."

"No. That's not what I meant. On the contrary. You've given me an idea. I'm free this morning. I'm going to visit her at her salon. That way I can get some fresh air and stray beyond the Tuscolano neighborhood."

Tania beams.

"Good, she'll be so pleased."

"I have to do something first, though."

His mother understands. She gives her son a kiss and leaves the room.

He hurries to his charging smartphone. He checks his calls, then the chat.

Camilla has not been in touch since last night's sorrowful "Good night."

Gabriele starts writing a message.

Dear Cam, I miss you so much. If you want,
I'll even come back up now. Your doctor is right:
if you're not careful, you can drown in an empty glass.

Right now I feel like the guy inside the glass.
I'm just asking for a little time. Call me.
Write to me. Don't leave me hanging.

Camilla is online. She reads the message. Gabriele waits, hoping that the notification that she is writing appears on his display.

But nothing happens.

After reading, she closes the chat.

Gabriele travels along Viale Palmiro Togliatti in a taxi.

This thoroughfare connects the south of Rome to the east.

From Tuscolano all the way to Tiburtino.

The suburbs it runs through, built in the '70s and '80s, used to be the city's dirty, working-class boundaries. Now they are semicentral, desirable neighborhoods compared to the miles of buildings that have risen up over time far beyond the limits of the Grande Raccordo Anulare highway, turning the capital into an endless metropolis, an unstoppable flow that has devoured hectares and hectares of countryside. One after another the towns that once served as its border have effectively become the city's new, more remote outskirts.

The Centocelle district teems with languages and colors.

A multi-ethnic environment, always wavering between peaceful coexistence and mutual distrust.

The cab stops at the address Gabriele gave the driver. A side street off Via Casilina. He pays and gets out.

He approaches his sister's salon.

He does not quite understand.

The sign: "Giorgia hair stylist."

And the interior with armchairs and mirrors.

Everything as he saw it in the photos taken on the opening day.

Too bad the roller shutter is down and there are piles of mail lying everywhere, not to mention dirt that looks like it has been accumulating for some time.

He notices he is being watched; across the sidewalk, in front of his store, a Chinese man is smoking a cigarette.

"Sorry, is it closed?"

Gabriele realizes that it was a stupid question; sure enough, the guy does not give any kind of answer.

"I meant, how long has it been closed for?"

The man extends his hand and holds up a finger.

"A month?"

He shakes his head.

"A year?"

An affirmative nod.

Gabriele is stunned. He stares at the Chinese man, who returns his stare. He would like to ask him why, because now, all of a sudden, the few certainties of his life have begun to falter, or rather, to completely crumble.

But the Chinese guy has finished his cigarette and returned to his store.

Another taxi drives along Togliatti in the opposite direction.

From east to south.

"Hello? Gabriele?"

"Hi. You weren't at dinner last night and I wanted to know if everything was okay."

"Yeah, yeah, I'm at the salon. It's a pretty busy day. See you tonight, bro. A customer is about to pay so I've got to go now."

Gabriele was not familiar with this pain.

The pain of discovering betrayal.

Up until now he belonged to the category of traitors, of small acts, just enough to live without ever really facing life.

A low-level traitor, mind you.

Via Selinunte runs through half of Quadraro.

The cab drops him off opposite one of the many low-rise, pleasant-looking tenement buildings that face the street.

The gate is open.

So is the building's front door.

This allows him to reach his sister's door without even pressing a doorbell so he can present himself with the anger that has mounted from the phone call with her onward, in the hope that she will be home . . .

He rings.

The noises leave no doubt.

Giorgia opens and, seeing her brother, she smiles. Then it dawns on her and the smile fades. Her eyes drop and her face turns to the floor.

"Why?"

"Come in. I don't want the whole building to hear."

A two-room apartment of about five hundred square feet, furnished with love; taste is another matter.

"Why?"

Gabriele repeats the question.

Giorgia, after an initial collapse, has recovered. She looks her brother in the eye, trying to keep her emotions under control.

"Why? I went bust. That's all. It's impossible to compete with the Chinese and Indians. They do a cut and blow dry for twelve euros. I held out as long as I could. Then it got to a point where my expenses were four times higher than my takings, and I closed. Happy?"

"Why didn't you tell me? Do you think I wouldn't have understood? It's difficult to start any kind of business, especially in times like these. You just had to tell me."

Giorgia bursts into laughter that spills into tears.

"Sure. I just had to tell you. I just had to tell the world that Giorgia Bilancini, after her studies and her marriage, has failed yet another of life's trials. After all, it was always you who won for both of us. You were the winner, and I was the loser. Ever since we were kids."

"So not even Mom and Dad know?"

Giorgia wipes her eyes with the cuff of her sweater and shakes her head.

"I felt ashamed. With you. With them. The truth, Gabriele, is that your sister isn't worth shit."

Her brother instinctively hugs her and holds her close. This contact makes her bend forward in despair.

"I'm forty years old and I've done nothing. Nothing. You don't know what that means."

"Of course I know. I know what shame and loneliness mean. Nostalgia. Winning doesn't make you happy, Giorgia. I'm not so different from you."

She suddenly pulls away.

"What are you talking about? You fulfilled the dream you had as a child. You became a celebrity. How can you say you're like me?"

"I mean that I also live with many unspoken things, lies. I'm an asshole in many ways. You're all convinced that success makes people better than they are, but that's not true. You stay what you are. If you don't get worse. With guilt eating away at you."

When she hears him mention guilt, Giorgia bursts into tears again.

"Please. Please don't tell Mom and Dad. I'll find a job as soon as possible. As soon as I sort myself out, you don't have to give me that money anymore. I kept quiet about that too. But how could I pay for this house without money? The bills? I would've had to go back to Mom and Dad like a little girl who can't accomplish anything by herself."

"Giorgia, money is the last thing on my mind. It makes no difference to me whether I'm helping you with a hair salon or to live. As long as you need me, I'll be there no matter what. But promise me that you won't give up and you'll try again. Because you're so talented. When I was a kid, I used to watch you and envy you: the way you talked, how clever you were. Just one thing: promise me that you won't think of yourself as a nobody anymore. Will you promise me that?"

Giorgia, her eyes swimming with tears, nods to her brother.

"Okay."

Gabriele kisses her on one cheek.

"Of course, it will stay a secret between you and me. Like when we were kids and grandma's vase got broken by a gust of wind."

"When it was actually us."

"Exactly."

"Thanks, Gabriele. I don't know what else to say."

"You don't have to say anything. Will I see you tonight with Mom?"

His sister tries to smile.

She looks like a survivor.

A woman who has recovered from a disaster that only damaged her face.

2

It is an abnormal April.

If indeed there is anything normal left about the climate. For a thousand and one reasons, Rome has become a city that more closely resembles a North African capital than its European counterparts.

In summer, the temperature now scarcely differs from the land across the Mediterranean. What the Romans used to call the 'ponentino'—the westerly breeze that lightened the mugginess a little in the evenings—is a distant memory.

Gabriele is walking through Parco degli Acquedotti.

His phone vibrates in his pocket. He pulls it out, hoping, praying that his Camilla's name is on the display. Instead, it is his mother.

"Everything okay, Gabriele?"

"Yes. Why?"

"It's one thirty. I wasn't sure if you were coming and . . . "

"One thirty?"

He cannot believe it.

"Yeah, Mommy has made you a salad. I put . . . "

"Sorry, Mom, I won't make it in time. The morning has flown by and I'm still far from home."

"How was your sister? Did you see how much work she has?"

"Yeah. I saw. She's really good. I'll talk to you later, I'm in a store."

"Speak later, darling."

Gabriele slips the phone into his pocket. As he was speaking, he reached Casale di Roma Vecchia, a historic building in the park. There is a little pond next to it known as the 'Laghetto', but it is shrunken and dried up compared to how he remembered it. Not far away is one of the aqueducts that cross this patch of land still untouched by concrete. He tries to remember. As a kid, he knew all their names by heart.

This must be the famous Aqua Marcia aqueduct, or is it Anio Vetus? He no longer remembers as he used to.

He only knows one thing.

One summer twenty years ago, when they were both little more than teenagers, he and Vanessa made love just behind these ancient brick arches.

They lost their virginity right there.

On one side, memories, the enticing spring bursting around him, the beauty of the places he loved; on the other, the misery he chose for himself, because no one ever forced him to lie, to be ashamed, to put everything into a hierarchy.

Gabriele wants to cry but is simply unable to.

He is now living in a state of disenchantment.

Things can never be fixed. At least not for him. He does not have the strength, the ability. It takes character and strong hands, and he is weak.

There is only one thing he wants.

To return to enchantment.

What he experienced as a young boy.

What made him believe in the great dream that he had to achieve.

And they all lived happily ever after.

But no.

The earth keeps spinning and crushing.

There is no place nor price.

When the enchantment broke, it broke.

You can only lose once.

Like the virginity consummated with Vanessa, right where he is standing now, right here, all those years ago.

What remains of what we have experienced? The memory. And the pain of recalling it: nostalgia.

It travels through time and space.

Gabriele keeps walking, stopping on a perfect clump of grass that looks like it was cut with scissors by a barber.

He spontaneously feels like lying down.

The April sunshine caresses him. At least the sun does not seem to judge him.

There is an earthquake.

He sees the buildings in the distance collapsing one by one.

Then he wakes up.

It was the vibration of his phone ringing in his pocket that ignited his imagination; not the lucid, conscious kind, but dreamlike, uncontrollable thoughts.

His heart is still pounding from anxiety at being duped by his dream.

Someone is calling him.

Once again, it is not Camilla.

"I stopped by your house. Your mom told me you were out and about. Where have you got to?"

Gabriele drowsily listens to Marcello's voice. Perhaps now he is really starting to worry about his girlfriend's silence.

"I'm here in the park, taking a walk."

"We're all at the bar."

"Christ, you live like Bill Murray in *Groundhog Day*."

Gabriele would like to tell him this.

"I'll join you."

"Great, bro."

Gabriele's phone lingers in his hand.

He opens the chat with Camilla.

He types.

Please give me a smile.

A few moments pass, then she reads it. This time the notification that she is writing appears. This alone fills Gabriele with joy.

How can I show you? You know I don't like
photos taken with a smartphone.

He replies without thinking.

I don't need to see it.
You only need to smile and I'll know.

I'm smiling.

Can we make up, Chamomile?
If you want I'll leave now.
I'll walk to Milan.

I did a lot of thinking last night.
I wasn't able to listen, to understand.
I'm still angry with you, but I haven't
experienced certain things. But promise
me that we'll work through
all this shit together.

Of course. I promise you.

You've told me so much about
your family, your friends.
Why should I care about anything else?
Love is love.
Let's leave aesthetic judgment to Milan.

I couldn't live without you.
I love you, Camilla Chamomile.
I really missed telling you.

I love you so very much, my Roman boy.
I missed it too. Speak tonight.

OK. A kiss. Many.

Gabriele sets off.
It is as if he took some quick-relief medicine.
His shortness of breath instantly vanished.

3

He sees them from a distance.

Always at the same table.

Always the same group.

Marcello, Cristiano, Francesco, and Vanessa.

Gabriele, as he approaches, does not know whether to laugh or cry.

"Hey, where did you disappear to?"

"Lello old fellow, you won't believe it. I reached the Casale di Roma Vecchia, sunbathed a little and fell asleep like a log."

He sits down with them.

"If you'd called me, I would've come and joined you. I would've had a nice doze in the sun too."

"What a hard life you lead, huh. While I was wrapping trolley after trolley."

Cristiano puffs out cigarette smoke as he speaks. With his complexion and pointed face, he almost looks like a dragon.

"Will you have a spritz, too?"

Vanessa asks Gabriele with her usual smile.

"Gladly."

"You know when you feel like you've forgotten something, but you can't think what?"

Marcello is lost in some unclear thoughts, at least so he says. He snaps his fingers.

"I've got it. We were talking about depression yesterday. Francesco was feeling a little sick and we ended up discussing this cheerful topic."

He spoke looking at Vanessa, the only one who was absent at the same table the previous day. She glares at him, making no attempt to hide her annoyance at the mention of this subject.

"And in the end, I said that pretty much all of us here suffer from depression, except for Cristiano, who makes other people depressed. You too, Vanessa, what do you take? Zoloft? Cymbalta?"

"Lello, you didn't just stay small in height; your brain stayed small too, like a seven-year-old boy. An eight-year-old at best."

Vanessa, flushed with embarrassment, does not know where to look.

"It's true. I haven't been very well. After the divorce, anyway. I've started to cut down on my meds now."

Marcello realizes that he was being tactless.

"Sorry, I didn't think it was confidential."

"Well, you know, treatment with psychiatric drugs. Am I supposed to hold up a sign?"

He shrugs.

"I'll stop talking. Ah, another thing . . . "

"Didn't you say you'd stop talking? Shut up for five minutes. You sound like a radio."

Francesco, from his other world, slowly pronounced these words, his face directed at the sun. He turns to Gabriele and looks at him with his eyes still haunted by sorrow.

"I wanted to apologize for yesterday, Gabriele. It's just that when I see a ball again, it's like showing a syringe to a junkie."

"You don't have to apologize, Francesco. We both went too far."

Each of Francesco's smiles seems to be his last, and perhaps he would like it to be. A farewell, final smile to this life that so deluded him and then betrayed him forever.

Everyone at the table enjoys this little moment of reconciliation, of reestablished, reciprocated friendship, like when children make up.

"Anyway, Lello, seriously, change your meds. Get one that makes you shut up at least every fifteen minutes and say something smart one time in ten."

Cristiano lunges, and Marcello takes the hit, but carries on as if nothing happened:

"I wanted some advice, but it doesn't matter."

He leaves these words hanging in the air. Gabriele cannot resist.

"Then ask, Lello old fellow."

He perks up.

"Thanks, Gabriele. One of you is still nice, thank God. Nothing. In two weeks, I have to go to a christening. It's the daughter of my cousin, the one in Casal Bruciato. Do you think I have to wear a jacket? Mom says yes, but I don't feel comfortable in a jacket. I'd rather go in a linen shirt, especially in this heat."

"Sure, what's wrong with that? Nowadays, even at ceremonies everyone dresses as they like."

Gabriele answered without thinking, conscious that his reply sounds trite. Marcello, however, takes his words at face value.

"Perfect. It's a baptism after all, not a wedding. Speaking of baptisms, last night I was thinking that none of us have had kids. We need to keep up the Italian birth rate!"

It was meant to be a joke. But he is the only one laughing.

The table plunges into a kind of vacuum.

Vanessa's expression has changed. Cristiano too. Now his eyes are frighteningly mean.

"You have the body of an eight-year-old, but your brain would barely make it to kindergarten. You've got the brain of a three-year-old. I'm going to piss. Otherwise, if I keep talking, you'll end up crying." He gets up and goes inside the bar.

Marcello makes himself smaller than he is.

Vanessa looks at him with a mix of severity and compassion.

"Lello old fellow, why are you such a dumbass? No wonder

that Romanian . . . What was her name? Helena? The one who looked like a Picasso painting. That's why she left you."

"It's okay, Lello, it happens. We all talk without thinking sometimes. Don't take it to heart."

Gabriele tries to console him too.

"Too bad it's been happening to him every day for thirty-five years."

They try not to react to these words from Francesco, who is still facing the sun, but cannot help themselves.

Vanessa and Gabriele start laughing.

Marcello eventually follows suit.

It is as if he has been reborn. He seems to feed on his friends' happiness. The words that were launched just a second earlier no longer exist for him.

"It's so nice when we all laugh."

4

"No more spritz, or I won't remember the way home." Marcello finishes the last sip from his glass. The mood is jolly again; everyone is in high spirits, or perhaps it would be more accurate to say tipsy.

"Still, you're right about one thing. Milan. It's beautiful. Everything works. But at night it's like there's a curfew at nine o'clock. You have to go into bars, otherwise everywhere is a desert, or rather a tundra."

"I'm just saying, it's half past seven in the evening and we're still out in the sun. The Romans knew what they were doing when they chose this area."

Vanessa, feeling the effects of the alcohol, has even more glazed eyes when she talks to Gabriele.

"Help a brother out. Hey, gorgeous, do you want a bracelet?"

The quintet is interrupted by an elderly black man, smiling, trying to sell the usual trinkets along with bracelets, small wooden key chains, and elephant-shaped figurines.

Vanessa shakes her head and turns her gaze back to the table.

"Want to buy a bracelet, bro? It brings good luck!"

Francesco does not even answer him.

"How about you? You look like you're from my country. You're African. Want to buy something?"

Cristiano shakes his head.

"No, we already told you. And I'm not from your country."

"Bro! I'm telling you, you're from my country . . . "

"I said I'm not from your country and I'm sure as hell not your 'bro'. Now get the fuck out of here. Got it?"

The peddler takes the hint and immediately leaves. Cristiano watches him walk away.

"These fucking niggers."

Vanessa, Marcello, and Francesco do not react; just by looking at them, you can tell that this judgment, those words, are, if not endorsed, certainly usual.

"Why?"

Gabriele, on the other hand, is shocked, distressed.

"Why what?"

"Why did you treat him like that? Why?"

When he is totally serious, as he is right now, Cristiano is frightening.

"Come on, don't start playing the saint now. You used to call them that too, didn't you?"

"We were just stupid children. I needed to travel the world. I've met African guys who know five or six languages and graduated in spite of all the hardship. I can tell you they're much more cultured than us Italians. Guys who are not afraid of anything. Cosmopolitan, free."

A fake, amateur actor's laugh.

Cristiano regards provocation as an art form.

"More cultured than us. I haven't heard that one before. Well, it had to come out sooner or later. I was waiting for this. You're the one who has seen the world, who succeeded. Us assholes just stayed here. Oh well, it can't be helped. We've stayed ignorant. We've even got bitter."

"I'm not saying this because I've been successful, but because I've seen how things work elsewhere, how . . . "

"Sorry to interrupt, but I want to tell you how things work around here. For years now, not one fucking thing has worked here. They make you feel like it's you against everyone and everything. With no help and no future. Just with a whole new set of commandments. And if you don't respect them, you go to hell. You can't call a nigger a nigger anymore. Same with faggots. Well, you know what I, or actually we, do? We do the opposite of what people like you say."

"Calm down, Cristiano."

Vanessa tries to intervene, but he does not even look at her.

"Who do you mean people like me?"

Gabriele does not back down.

"You know who I mean. The good guys. It's like a rule: the more money you make, the more saintly you get. But I want to be bad because no one has ever defended me, my dad, my mum, my siblings. No one. I want to be the exact opposite of what you are. Are you on the left? Then I'm on the right. Yeah. Actually, I'll go one step further. I'm a fascist. For people like you I'll always be ugly, dirty, and bad. So, I might as well be genuinely bad."

"I first came here when they were erecting these buildings."

It is Signor Antonio's voice. He is standing by the table carrying an empty tray. He makes everyone turn around.

"Up until those years, what is now a beautiful park was an expanse of shacks and starving people looking for work, all from the South. In order to eat, they used to steal and prostitute themselves. There was a priest, Don Sardelli, who taught them to write and read. He even moved to live in the slum."

He looks at the five of them sitting at the table, fighting back tears.

"But this neighborhood has an older history. My father was one of the guys caught in the Quadraro round-up in '44. Two thousand men and boys were arrested and taken away. Almost seven hundred never returned. They were sent to Germany and died there. My father was lucky. After a night of torture in Cinecittà he managed to escape. He made it home just in time."

Signor Antonio dries his eyes with the dirty rag that he uses to wipe the tables.

"He came home. He was sick. In a bad state. We were just kids. They made him drink a whole bottle of castor oil with a funnel. He died like an animal with his guts spilling out of his . . . And today, a lifetime later, I still have to listen to people talking about these things."

He looks at Cristiano with absolute contempt.

"That's why I'm leaving, why I sold everything. I don't want to die here. There's a nastiness in the air that I haven't felt for years. These days, the poor tear each other to shreds, and the poorer you are, the more they despise you. If these aqueducts could talk, they'd always say the same thing. That man never learns."

Signor Antonio, with his crooked gait, leaves without taking away the empty glasses.

Cristiano felt his words like a slap. He looks at Gabriele with hatred.

"Anyway, I've figured you out. I've taken a photo of you, like the one where it looks like you're kissing your boss."

"That's enough, Cristiano."

"Yeah, come on Cristiano, stop it."

Vanessa and Marcello try to calm him down to no avail. Francesco has totally isolated himself; he no longer seems present.

"You feel like you're this bigshot now. You treat us as ignorant losers. Just sitting with us is a struggle for you. It's not like you're one of us anymore; you belong to another breed now, right? Us. This place. The truth is that it all disgusts you. You're ashamed of what you used to be. Just say it."

Vanessa rests a hand on Cristiano's arm.

"Stop it, Cristiano, you're making me feel sick."

He jerks away from her.

"I'm done. I've only got one thing left to say to a guy who used to be a friend. Always remember: you're Gabriele Bilancini, son of Mauro the Fish, a mechanic who fixes motorcycles and scooters, not even cars. And always remember that to a rich guy, a truly rich guy, the kind who has always been rich, you'll always just be a bum, a guy who has talent for some reason but will never measure up to them."

Gabriele gets up without a word.

He starts to head home.

"Gabriele!"

Marcello and Vanessa try to call him back, but he does not stop. He is offended of course, but he left for another reason. If he went back, he could only tell Cristiano one thing.

"You're right. You're right about everything."

The photo he took of him is strikingly accurate.

5

"For your last night, I had to make the dish that I can respectfully call my proudest creation. Tradition is tradition, after all. Carbonara. The authentic kind."

The complete Bilancini family is gathered around the table.

The reaction is not particularly enthusiastic. Tania realizes this and interrogates her kin with her eyes.

"What's the matter with you all? What happened? Especially you two. You look down in the dumps."

She addresses her children.

Her husband, by contrast, seems to be waiting for his portion with obvious appetite.

"We better eat, or it'll get cold. The last night is becoming more like the Last Supper."

Mauro the Fish delivered the usual wry remark.

"I'll answer for Giorgia."

Gabriele starts talking and at the same time grabs the plate his mother has filled for him.

"I was at the salon today. She works flat out. She's just tired. She should eat and hit the sack."

"Yeah."

So many things pass from the sister's eyes to her brother's: complicity, the feeling of sharing a secret, boundless gratitude.

"How about you? You look really fed up."

Tania stares at him as he sits down to start eating.

"What can I say? The reason I stayed on here—Cristiano's invitation—may not be valid anymore. Let's say we had a little argument."

"What happened?"

His mother immediately fires up.

"A nasty fight. It all started because a peddler came by, and Cristiano insulted him because he was black. I'm not putting up with that."

"It's slowly collapsing. This municipality is still holding up, but the surrounding districts are in a dire state. The more poverty starves people, the more it risks making them cruel. Unfortunately, the world has begun to spin the wrong way: it's going backward instead of forward."

"It's like your father says. That's the problem. Don't forget that out of all of you, Cristiano is the one who comes from the poorest family. They went through years when they had to choose between lunch or dinner. I'm not saying you should agree with him, just that you have to understand where all that anger comes from. It'll all work out, you'll see."

Gabriele does not respond. He eats the carbonara with his eyes downcast.

"As usual, my compliments to the chef."

He smiles at his mother.

But she does not seem as pleased as usual.

She is upset and cannot hide it.

She regards the quarrel between her son and Cristiano as a personal defeat.

Only the father and son are left at the table.

Giorgia, as soon as she finished eating, wished everyone good night and went off to sleep.

So did Tania. After preparing a banana and apple fruit salad, she said good night and retired to bed.

"I feel worn-out this evening," she said before shutting herself in her room.

Mauro and Gabriele are sipping an amaro liqueur. They are silently looking out the window at Parco degli Acquedotti in its nighttime guise: a black expanse lit by a few streetlights in the area closest to Via Lemonia, then by other scattered lights; the rest is in the hands of darkness.

"I want to tell you something I've never told you. Your mother is one of the only people who knows."

"I swear I won't tell anyone."

"It's not like it's a secret. It's just that—you know me—I keep certain things to myself. Not because I'm selfish. I just don't speak much. Anyway, I don't have to explain to you what your father is like."

Mauro downs his last sip of amaro.

"As a boy, I loved motorcycles. One day they took me to the Vallelunga circuit. Aside from my marriage and your births, it was the best moment of my life. A distinguished gentleman, the head of a team, said I had the mind of a racer, of a professional. He left me his phone number."

"Then what?"

"Then nothing. I didn't have the courage to go to your grandparents and say: I want to ride motorcycles. But most of all I didn't believe it. That's the real problem. I thought: 'do you think the world will give Mauro Bilancini a chance?'. Now that we're alone, I can tell you: forget that you're my son, I admire you because you believed it, you had the strength. And you've shown me that if you try, if you try with all your passion, as you did, the world will give you a chance."

For a moment, Gabriele is able to view himself from outside.

His father confronted him with what he has accomplished from an objective standpoint, cleansed of the inner turmoil he experiences every day.

He gave him a clear, pure vision.

The son of a mechanic from Via Lemonia in the Tuscolano neighborhood, who becomes the surrogate son, the favorite pupil, of a contemporary design guru.

Who himself becomes a name in international design.

"Dad, you don't know how important those words are to me."

His father stands up.

"You, you're important. I just spoke the truth. I'm going to join your mother. Good night."

"Good night, Dad. Thanks again."

Gabriele is left alone at the table.

He would like to cement this state of mind within himself, to never let it slip away again.

But he knows it is impossible.

"Hi, Cam."

Gabriele is in bed, under the sheet, with the phone resting against his ear.

"My Roman boy. How's your vacation going? Are you done spouting paranoia?"

"Are you still angry?"

"Yeah, I got angry. I felt scared. Being with someone and then finding out that he's this way in one place and that way in another. But it's like I wrote to you: I haven't done what you've done. I haven't lived in such different places and environments. I've always been inside this house, unfortunately."

"Why do you say that? Did something happen?"

Camilla can be heard sipping.

"What are you drinking?"

"A glass of wine. Anyway, the usual thing happened. What happens when you're the daughter of a god incarnate who believes he commands the elements of nature and obviously everyone's life, starting with mine."

"Your dad. What did he do?"

"That's the fun part. Human eyes wouldn't even notice, but it's him we're talking about. He went crazy because the leather we received for some models was a slightly different Pantone color than usual. I thought it looked the same and he ended up calling the whole team. It was a kind of test to single out the biggest ass licker. Only three of them had the courage to say it was identical.

The others all agreed with him. In the end, he gave me a look to say 'you of all people'. But to me that fucking leather was the same color as always. He's becoming more and more overbearing as he gets older, never questioning himself. I can't stand him anymore."

"I'm sorry. Well, actually it's been a stormy afternoon here too. I had a row with Cristiano, the one who is turning forty tomorrow. We really lashed out at each other today. He treated a black man like shit, an elderly guy who passed by with bracelets and the usual junk. There's such a divide between me and them now in so many ways."

"That's awful. Fuck, he's a troglodyte."

"Earlier we talked about kids. No one from the group I grew up with has had any."

"Well, that's got nothing to do with us. I want a child. Half Milanese snob like me and half Roman loudmouth. Actually, let's get on with it, then maybe my father will soften up. Can you imagine Pop-Pop Franco Zardi?"

Gabriele laughs.

"Frankly, no."

"Exactly. I'm really the second child. He has a firstborn son named design. Everyone else is light years away."

Camilla's pain is audible.

"Listen, I should already be able to come back tomorrow. Anyway, I don't think I'm invited anymore. Part of me immediately thought: thank God."

"It's up to you. But try to make it up with him. After all, each of us has a past and present. If I didn't have the past, the time I spent with my mother, with you . . . "

She cannot go on.

"Don't be like that, Camilla. I'll be back on Sunday at the latest. These days have been a test for both of us. Ah, by the way, just so you know, my mother's talk about the penthouse was a pipedream. All it did was make the two of us argue. They sold it a week ago."

Yet another lie is spawned.

She sniffles.

"I really don't care. I just want you to come back. I'm going crazy alone here."

"My darling Camilla, I love you so much, you know."

"I know. And you know how important you are to me."

Gabriele puts his phone down and stares at the ceiling.

History, from generation to generation.

The lineage of nobles and the lineage of beggars.

Then all it takes is one act of love and the blood is intertwined.

A new branch of a family tree is created from nothing.

Nature is so simple: it unites without judgment.

By contrast, everything man has built is so unequal, created solely to divide, to brand.

He falls asleep with Camilla's face in his eyes.

V
Aqua Claudia Aqueduct

1

"Good morning."

Tania waits for Gabriele to wake up, then hands him the cup of coffee.

It makes you wonder how she filled her life in the years when her son was not at home, when he was far away. It seems as if her entire existence revolves around him.

"Morning, Mom. Thanks."

"Mommy wanted to ask you something. If you're not busy, I wanted to take you with me to go grocery shopping. We'll take a walk together, then I have to get water, so you can give me a hand. The crates are heavy."

"They really are, yeah. I hate them. Okay, gladly. I'll take a shower, and we'll go."

"There's a banana and apple on the kitchen table if you like."

Gabriele gets up.

He goes over to the pile of clothes his mother kept for him.

He chooses a Lee plaid shirt. It was one of his favorite pieces of clothes.

"Then I have to figure out if I'm going to this party or not. Honestly, regardless of what Cristiano might say, I don't feel like it anymore."

Tania does not seem to have heard.

"Did you know that Signor Franco's store—the one he runs with his wife—is still open? I always get my meat from them. It's one of the few stores that has survived. Take your time. I'm ready when you are."

Tania leaves her son alone.
A message notification.

Good morning, my Roman boy.
My father summoned me and granted me
his forgiveness; he did not even want me to kneel.
Praise be to Saint Zardi.

Good morning Camilla Chamomile.
My mother asked me to go grocery shopping with her.
I told her I probably won't go to Cristiano's party,
but she brushed it aside.
You can tell it matters to her.

Poor thing. If you can make a sacrifice,
the party will only take a few hours.
Try to make her happy.

Gabriele's thumbs hover in the air, then he writes:

Yes.

Speak later. Say hi from me. I love you, Roman boy.

I love you more, Camilla Chamomile.

The mother and son are in the Cinecittà covered market.

Tania wanders around as if she were in her own apartment. Every step is a "Hi, Tania!", "Tania, honey, I've got some sourdough bread, fresh from the oven."

She smiles at everyone and approaches a fruit and vegetable stand.

"Hey, Tiziana!"

She is addressing a fruit seller, who turns around and listens.

"If you give me the same chicory as last time, I'll come knocking at your door."

"Why, my love? It's from Frosinone, picked the day before, I swear. Isn't that your son? The famous one who makes furniture?"

"Not regular furniture. He's a designer. We only see these things in newspapers. How much does the chair you designed cost, Gabriele?"

He is embarrassed, but he sees how happy and proud his mom is.

"It depends on the colors and materials. But let's say it starts, well, from six thousand euros, more or less."

This is met by a stony silence.

Tiziana, the fruit seller, with a lit cigarette hanging out the side of her mouth, cannot believe it.

"Six thousand euros?! What's it made of? Solid gold? My son furnished his whole house for six thousand euros, including the baby's room."

"My dear Tiziana, the world is made up of many worlds. So long."

Tania removes her son from the frying pan. The two of them continue.

"Tania! Gabriele!"

Vanessa has appeared close by. As usual, she is meticulously made up. She goes over to them, and they embrace.

"Are you shopping too?"

"I was looking for some fish, but I haven't found much."

"There isn't much stuff on Saturdays. Tuesdays are the best. The other week I got some sea bream for nine euros a kilo."

Vanessa nods, her eyes occasionally glued to Gabriele's face.

"Darling, go and have coffee with Vanessa. I'll take care of this."

He is totally caught off guard.

"But . . . I thought you needed a hand. Also, with the crates of water."

"There are still a couple at home. I'll just get a few little things. Don't worry."

She does not give him time to answer. She gives Vanessa a kiss on the cheek and wanders off.

"Shall we go to Signor Antonio?"

"No. I'll take you to a really nice café near here."

Vanessa starts walking. Gabriele follows behind.

2

"We haven't had a moment to talk since you arrived. Alone, I mean."

Vanessa has chosen one of the outdoor tables of a recently renovated bar not far from Via Tuscolana. Again today, like yesterday and the day before, a benevolent sun warms them at the perfect temperature.

"If there's one thing I'd totally forgotten, it's the weather. Rome truly is blessed."

Gabriele spoke with his eyes closed, facing the light, with the expression of someone enjoying the gifts of nature.

"Like I told you, the ancient Romans knew what they were doing. Anyway, what's it like in Milan?"

Vanessa is far more eager to make conversation than he is.

"It's a different city, starting with the weather. But the real difference is the mindset. The Milanese—I'm talking about the ones I hang out with—feel that they are part of an important place where important things happen, in step with the world. And maybe that's true. I like it there. I'm doing the job I always dreamed of, and I have my partner there. The complications are more on a personal, human level, but outside of dreamland those problems exist everywhere."

"It's the exact opposite of Rome. For years it's been like living in a depressed city that no longer believes in anything and anyone. It's all gone downhill. How about here? This neighborhood, your old life. Don't you miss anything about it?"

She asked him in a whisper crushed by a thousand different feelings, from nostalgia to suffering to hope.

Gabriele looks at her; he loved Vanessa with the intensity of first love. He discovered sex with her. Together they experienced intimacy, pleasure and jealousy. Everything excessive and magnificent that happens in young love. They shared so much life.

"I don't miss anything, and I miss everything. I don't even know myself. These days have been a kind of shock. I have my memories here. Especially the ones with you. And with other friends. I have my family here. But what I love most and what I miss right now is in Milan. That's Camilla."

She makes a superhuman effort not to be engulfed by the words she just heard.

"But tell me about you. Marcello told me you work nearby?"

Gabriele tries to distract her from the obvious pain his answer has unleashed.

"Me?"

A sour laugh. As often happens, his rescue efforts make the situation worse.

"I'm a cashier at Lidl, next to Giulio Agricola metro station. I don't know if you're familiar with it."

He shakes his head.

"It's a fixed shift from 7 A.M. to 2 P.M., six days a week. Two Sundays at home and the other two in rotation at work."

"Do you have anyone aside from your friends?"

"No one and plenty. Plenty who undress you and vanish a second later. No one who has stayed."

"We're at a cursed age. We're no longer kids, but we're still not very adult. But things can change, Vanessa, you're still young, beautiful, fun. Don't make the error I often make: thinking as if you were a hundred years old. You can still do many things and love many people."

"Thanks."

She says this with her beautiful eyes full of gratitude.

"I sat down hoping for the impossible. I would've so loved

to end this chat with a kiss, in front of everyone, picking up where we left off. But those are a little girl's dreams."

Gabriele does not know what to say. He looks at her tenderly; he can feel the love he felt for her flickering inside him under yards of ash.

"Don't think about the past, Vanessa. If it holds you back, if it's just a dead weight, discard it. You have a bright future ahead of you. I know you'll find someone who loves you for who you are."

She nods and instinctively gives Gabriele a chaste caress of pure innocence that barely grazes his face.

"Hopefully. You left me for a greater love, one you always had. Design. Then you found Camilla. Who knows. Maybe someone who loves me more than anything will come along for me, too."

Vanessa stands up.

"I invited you, and I'm paying for the coffee, or else I'll start hitting you like when we were dating, and you know who wins."

Gabriele raises his hands, smiling.

"I remember, yeah."

He watches her as she enters the café, waiting her turn at the cash register.

"She is Vanessa Fortuna. In another life, prior to this one, she was the first thought when you woke up and the last thought before you fell asleep. You would've done anything for her. And you thought, for days, months and years, that she, Vanessa, would be the woman of your life. Of all your lives."

Gabriele feels a kind of dizziness.

Today she is a near stranger, standing in line to pay for his coffee.

3

Gabriele walks with his hands in his pockets.

He is uncertain about how he feels.

Empty, melancholic, or perhaps, more than anything, dazed.

To him, life seems to be a very fast animal; man chases after it, trudging along and observing its changes in direction, its frantic evolutions, but he is and will always remain behind.

And then there is the past. Everyone can play—with a pencil and a sheet of paper—at drawing the outline of their existence, the places and the people, the choices and the sacrifices, until they reach the brink of the present.

Whether it is from yesterday or today, nothing belongs to us.

He only knows one thing: he has never stopped serving his passion. That is all he knows. Everything that has happened, good or bad, he owes to the love that has always commanded him.

Drawing. Bringing visions that arose in his mind to life.

"Hey, why the long face? I've been waiting for you for half an hour."

Right outside his front door, Cristiano is leaning against a car with the ever-present cigarette in his mouth.

"You wait for someone when that someone knows they've arranged to meet you, but what if they don't know? Why didn't you call?"

"Guess what? I wanted to surprise you. Give me the satisfaction: was it a surprise?"

Gabriele smiles, shaking his head.

"Yeah, Cristiano, it was a surprise. A nice one."

He moves away from the car and joins Gabriele.

"Let's go to the park. We can sit on a bench."

They walk side by side toward the green expanse, heading toward the aqueducts.

They sit on a slightly shaded bench.

The sun has become an enemy; its rays burn now.

"We should really get our swimsuits out."

Cristiano comments to keep silence at bay; once it settles in, it is always hard to drive it away.

"I'll cut to the chase. You know me. I certainly won't take back what I said: I'm on the right. For this neighborhood, for this city that they they've destroyed, I'd like a general who can straighten things out again. And I'll always prefer Italians to Africans. I know you don't agree. But yesterday I shouldn't have treated that poor wretch like that. It's true what Signor Antonio said: now they make the poor tear each other apart."

"I don't know, Cristiano. I think the problem isn't those who have less, but those who have so much more, those who have too much and don't give a damn about anything. Those who pretend to feel pity but are actually monsters."

"Ah, you're talking about your friends, the ones who don't practice what they preach. The radical chic. But I don't want to talk about that. I'm also here because I wanted to explain to you that I was already feeling tense yesterday. From the moment that screwball Marcello started talking about kids."

For the first time Cristiano shows something akin to vulnerability, still enraged, but somehow resigned.

"A couple of years ago, I found out I'm infertile. I dreamed of having a large family. But no. They say the younger generations are in even worse shape."

He lights another cigarette. Gabriele grabs his knee and squeezes it.

"I'm sorry, Cris."

"Me too. Really sorry. And there's nothing I can do about it. Nothing."

It feels like jumping from a diving board without being able to see the water below or if there even is any.

Gabriele has to make a superhuman effort.

"Speaking of yesterday, I also . . . "

He does not have the strength to continue.

"What? Come on, we're alone. What we say to each other stays here."

"It's just about me. Yesterday, when you told me you'd taken a photo of me, many things you said are right. I've changed. It's true. I'm not like all of you anymore. I entered another world, and I had to adapt because otherwise that world devours you. I've had more fun these days than I've had in years, but at times I've also felt like . . . like an alien."

"You said it yourself the first day at Signor Antonio's bar: life takes us where it wants, and it makes us change. Unfortunately, or fortunately, that's the way it is."

"It's true, Cristiano. The problem is that I'm not like you anymore, but I'll never be like them. Like the people I hang around now. I've tried to imitate them. Many succeed. They believe in it so much that in the end they think they're the same breed. I've tried. There was a time when I actually wanted that, but I couldn't do it. Because . . . many of them disgust me. I hate them. You're right: behind the nice facade, they're still masters. They expect everything, often without the slightest courtesy."

"So how can you stand it? I mean, how can you stay there, turning a blind eye to it?"

"I really love the work I do, and Camilla is a great girl. She's a daughter of that world, but she's different. She lost her mother when she was thirteen; maybe, that's why. But it's still difficult. You should see them when they let their guard down, when they take off the mask that 'we're all the same'. They've put me down so many times. Because I didn't study like them at the Royal College of Art in London, or at Parsons in New York. You should see the way they look at me or how they laugh at certain things, the disgusted faces they make. 'It's an industrial product for poor people'."

Now Gabriele is the one pumping out anger to the point of tears.

"Well, what do you know."

"I live without a land, without a world. Everywhere I feel like I'm suspended."

"We thought you were rich and happy. You've got rich, damn you, but you still need to work on getting happy."

Cristiano accomplished what he wanted: to make Gabriele smile.

"Ah, you've got to tell me if I'm still welcome at your fortieth birthday party."

"If you don't come, I'll break your neck. And I don't mean to be petty, but you haven't wished me happy birthday."

"Happy birthday, Cristiano. I finally managed to talk to someone about what I'm going through. For the first time. Promise me it will stay between you and me."

"Dude, I still have secrets from when you were a kid. You know my lips are sealed. I'll expect you this evening at eight. A standing dinner and then some wild dancing. But did I tell you where it's going to be?"

Gabriele shakes his head.

"It took me a year. The place has theoretically been seized—it has been repossessed a few times—but I eventually managed it. Eight o'clock at LeGriffe."

"I don't believe it."

"Well, you better believe it. Do you remember the afternoons we spent in there?"

"Sure, I remember them."

The sun now fully illuminates the bench where they sat to talk.

"Take some of that and say hi to Milan for me."

"You know, the weather has changed up there."

"Who says it hasn't? It has become identical to Rome. The exact same."

They both laugh.

"I'm going to head home. Today is my last lunch with Mom. You can imagine just how delighted she'll be."

"I'm going to stay and soak up some sun. As of today, I'm forty years old. Vitamin D is important."

Gabriele gets up to leave and Cristiano stands up to say goodbye.

This time it feels like the first embrace after spending centuries apart.

4

Gabriele was not expecting this.

Everyone is sitting around the table.

"Your father hasn't come home for lunch in at least twenty years. And Giorgia closed the store for the occasion; she's normally open all day."

"What an honor. But there was no need."

"What do you mean? You leave tomorrow."

Tania says no more because she is unable to; her words are swollen with emotion.

"Don't be like that, Ta."

Her husband spoke in a different voice than usual, drier, harsher.

"Yeah, Mom, he's leaving, but it's not like he's off to the front line. He's going to Milan; it's a three-hour train ride away."

"Okay, okay. You're right. I'm overreacting. I'll stop now and we can eat."

Tania sits down, trying to obey her family's entreaties.

"It's true. The train only takes three hours from here. It's not like he's going to war."

She repeats this to herself, trying to convince herself while attempting to smile.

"Ah and remember that thing I told you. Think about it."

Her beautiful eyes momentarily drift to the penthouse for sale. Only the mother and son understand.

Gabriele, sitting beside her, hugs her.

"Mom, I have colleagues from Scandinavia and Brazil. We're

just a stone's throw away. And I've promised you I'll come back. And I also promise you that I'll think seriously about that thing . . . "

The chair he is sitting on, or rather, the floor where the chair stands, suddenly seems to be made of earth. Swampy, unstable ground.

Gabriele finds himself sinking.

He has no intention of coming back more often.

Let alone of buying a house in the neighborhood.

These days have been the ultimate proof that the chasm in which he exists—the lands of his past and present—are meant to remain where they are, separated by an unbridgeable distance.

"God will punish me for lying to my mother."

This echoes in his head as she, granting his every wish like an order, or even an honor, places a salad with grilled chicken on the table; the chicken has been cut into tiny cubes with the skill that only lovers possess.

"Cristiano buzzed earlier. He was looking for you."

"He waited for me down here. We had a chat, and we made it up. Or rather, we came to a compromise."

Gabriele has a mouthful of salad and cannot continue; he drinks a glass of water to help it down.

"He certainly hasn't changed his political views all of a sudden. Neither have I. He tried to explain himself though. We told each other things that will stay between us. It's like you said, Mom: he has a lot of anger for understandable reasons."

Naturally, Gabriele says nothing about what he himself spewed out.

"So, are you going to the party tonight?"

"Yes, all confirmed."

"I'm so glad! And how did it go with Vanessa?"

Tania does her best to disguise the tension with which she threw out the last question. It is precisely her feigned lack of interest—so unnatural, so out of place for someone like her—that plants a suspicion in her son.

"Now that you ask, for some reason I'm starting to think that it wasn't such a chance encounter this morning, that someone's little hand was behind it. Someone who set it all up nicely."

"Surely, you're not thinking of me?"

"Yeah, Mom, you're exactly who I'm thinking of."

It is not so rare to see adults turn back into children.

Gabriele's insinuation is affectionate, with no acrimony, but rather, if anything, with the state of mind of someone who realizes, once again if proof were needed, how much he is loved by those he has beside him. But he notices how embarrassed his mother is.

"Whatever. It doesn't matter. Anyway, it went the only way it could go. I told her about Camilla. She told me about what she does, about her life now. Rather than coffee, we each drank half a liter of nostalgia. But the past is the past. It was nice, though. I mean to see her again and talk to her properly, alone."

Tania nods.

She does not respond in any way, either through words or her facial expression.

Giorgia listened to everything without saying anything.

Meanwhile, Mauro looked at his wife the whole time with infinite melancholy.

But his rule of silence prevails.

Hi Cam, what are you doing?

I had lunch with Dad. I'm resting now,
then a Chinese delegation is arriving at 5.
The trustees of a fund. From what
we understand they are about
to acquire one of those gigantic hotel chains
and they're coming to take a look.

What does your Dad say?

What can he say?
He has dressed in black. In mourning.
You know he's terrified of Chinese
and Arab people. Some of them are reasonable,
but others want everything right away
and just how they say.

I made it up with Cristiano.
I'm going to the party tonight.
Tomorrow morning I'll take
the Frecciarossa direct to Milan.
It leaves around 10.

I'm glad you've patched things up,
even if he's a fascist.

We talked a lot this morning.
But of course those are his views
and neither of us took a step back.
But he has many reasons to be pissed off.

All I care about is that you're here
with me tomorrow.

Exaaaactly.

Roman boy, when you get here tomorrow,
I'm going to devour you like an olive.
I'll only leave the stone.

Gabriele bursts out laughing. He types an answer.

You're crazy. I'm not going to call you Chamomile anymore, but Carnal Camilla.

Nice. And get ready. I mean physically. I'll say goodbye now. The studio phone is ringing. Bye, my love.

Bye, my darling darling Camilla.

Gabriele, lying on the bed, closes his eyes and lets his imagination run free. He finds Camilla naked beside him.

For a little while he lets himself be seduced, then he tries to dispel the vision.

He lies on his side, his favorite sleeping position.

He has had this habit since childhood, following his mother's example of switching off in the afternoon for at least half an hour. That rest makes his afternoon work more enjoyable and productive. He is convinced of this, although he often feels that it is just a habit that stems from his upbringing. Now, however, whether it is genuinely restorative or not, he must lie down and doze; he needs an escape in sleep.

His vibrating phone seems unwilling to let him have his way. He looks at the display: Marcello.

"Homeboy, I heard that you and Cristiano worked things out. I'm so happy."

He speaks in a very loud voice; Gabriele has to move the smartphone away from his ear.

"They've delegated me. Actually, as usual I'm their stooge. Anyway, I'm going to Via Tuscolana at six to look for a gift. I'd be glad if you come with me since you've got good taste. I mean, who better than you. Then we'll go straight to LeGriffe."

"Lello old fellow, you need to check your phone first. You might perforate some eardrums. It sounds like you're yelling."

"I *am* yelling! I'm in the subway. It's crazily full. You wouldn't believe the mess."

"Okay. I'll meet you in front of your house at five. Now I'm going to hang up or I might lose my hearing."

"Bye, bro."

Gabriele shakes his head. Marcello should be held up as a living example of tragicomedy.

He lies back on his side for his afternoon nap.

Someone knocks on the door. They seem to be doing it deliberately.

It is his mother with a pristine, freshly ironed white shirt.

"I thought for tonight . . . do you remember this shirt? You only wore it once."

"Honestly, no."

"Your sister's marriage. It wasn't just your shirt that met a sad end. But we mustn't dwell on that."

"Perfect. Just leave it hanging up."

"Have a good nap."

Tania goes out and closes the door. Gabriele, just in case, puts his phone in airplane mode.

Now he is unreachable. Until recently, this situation made him feel anxious.

He has slowly changed his mind.

Now he loves it, more and more every day.

5

It is certainly not a pleasant surprise.

On the contrary, it floods him with melancholy.

Even if, prior to his move, a negative trend was already apparent, as is the case in every city and town in Italy.

Gabriele walks alongside Marcello.

Via Tuscolana, which for decades was Rome's busiest shopping street, shows dismaying signs of decay. Many, many stores have closed.

"Do you remember what it was like when we were kids?"

While Gabriele is melancholic, Marcello's face is a mask of sorrow.

"We used to walk on these sidewalks and feel like we were the center of the world."

"Lello old fellow, everything has changed. The world. Customs. Us. Nothing is the same anymore."

"Let's change subject otherwise I'll get sad. I told you I'm on meds. What with my mom being sick and the neighborhood in this state, it feels like everything is turning into a desert."

"Have you thought what to give Cristiano?"

"No, that's why I brought you."

"Well, if they made you their stooge and chose you to come and get the gift, does that make me the stooge's stooge?"

Marcello gives a cheeky smile.

"Surely your taste can't be compared with . . . "

"Yeah, yeah, you already made your point."

Gabriele had not noticed it before; he pauses to take a closer look at the T-shirt his friend is wearing. Dark gray, all creased, with slanted white writing: "Balenciaga."

"Lello, can I ask you something? But promise me you won't get upset."

"I promise."

"Why do you buy these T-shirts from China? I don't want to get into aesthetics. But T-shirts like this—from these kinds of brands, which I honestly don't like—cost a monstrous amount."

"Yeah, mine is phony."

"You don't say? That's what I mean. Why do you have to wear a T-shirt that is obviously fake? Don't you think that's a slap in the face to this neighborhood? To the stores that have closed, to everyone who lives here. The real T-shirt costs a worker's salary."

"Well, I tell *you* it's phony, but if a girl came up to me, it's not like I'd tell her. I'd flaunt it as if it were real. There are only three options, Gabriele: be rich, be poor, or be poor and pretend to be rich. Then there are the rich who play at being poor, but they've never shown up around here. Today at least they give you this chance: imitate those who have money. Which, if you think about it, has always been a thing. Do you remember when they started selling fake Lacoste on Via Lemonia? The crocodile looked like an iguana."

"Holy shit, I'd forgotten."

They both start to laugh.

There is a jewelry store a few yards away from them. They are about to enter, but Marcello has something to say and stops.

"Bro, for Cristiano's fortieth we've pitched in a lot of money. A hundred each. I wanted to tell you. I don't think you have financial problems, but still a hundred euros is a hundred euros."

"Okay."

Gabriele looks at his friend.

Layers of human feelings slide one on top of the other.

Tenderness overlaid with compassion.

Then pride crushed by guilt.

"Look at that bracelet."

"The one with the anchor?"

"No, the one next to it. The one with the mesh that you tie up."

"I see it! So, you found it all by yourself, Lello. I think it's gorgeous!"

The white gold bracelet has a very fine double mesh that weaves back on itself in the center, creating a striking knot.

A 'Carrick bend', according to the tag beside it, which lists its various features.

It produces a tangled effect.

Like a kind of endless knot.

Gabriele, having initially liked it, now looks at it with annoyance. He would certainly never wear it, but he says nothing.

Marcello's eyes are sparkling.

"It's like our friendship."

"True, it's like all of you."

He turns sharply to Gabriele.

"You mean 'us', not 'you'."

"No, Lello old fellow, I don't live here anymore. You've actually built a life together."

"What's that supposed to mean? Of course you're part of it. In all our memories."

"Come on, let's go inside and buy that bracelet. It's getting late."

Gabriele did not answer so as not to hurt him.

His thinking about this has evolved as well. He cannot say exactly whether it is for better or worse.

Honoring memories until they become a creed.

Why? To what end?

He no longer understands its purpose.

He does not gain anything from it.

You cannot live with your head turned backward.

The past, if it becomes a dead weight, must be dropped, as he suggested to Vanessa this morning. Of course, he is not saying that it should be erased; he would not want that even if it were possible, which it is not. Anyway, it is fine to go back to it once in while in your mind and heart.

But you cannot turn the present into something accessory, secondary, minor, compared to devotion to what has been. No. He can understand this for someone who has reached the end of their life, with the best now behind them.

But he will not accept this from them; they are still young, after all.

Besides, the price of remembering is paid in nostalgia.

And he, since coming home, has spent a fortune.

6

The large red sign with “LeGriffe” in italics is no longer there.

The gate remains, now eaten away by rust.

The descent, which has always been steep, has filled with damp over the years of neglect; on the sides it is even covered with green moss, so anyone entering has to take care when going down.

The black entrance door is still there.

As teenagers they crossed it as if it were the threshold of the underworld, excited and frightened at the same time.

The club, after the entrance with a cloakroom, had a dance hall with sofas and small tables on either side. A corridor led to a room reserved for members, closed by a security door, a place inaccessible to them. Inside were the grown-ups with their gaming tables and deals. They often saw them leave at the pinnacle of happiness or devastated as if a relative had died. Various rumors—whether true or not—reached them: “He gambled away the store, and lost,” “You know the gas station behind Don Bosco, now it has another owner,” “The jeweler on Castro Street even bet his wife.”

When Gabriele and Marcello arrive, the line to enter starts at the gate on the road.

“Wow, Cristiano really went all out. He must’ve taken out some kind of loan.”

“Yeah, I didn’t expect so many people. There must be a hundred here.”

"I feel like I'm at the stadium turnstiles. Talking of which, if tomorrow you want . . . What the fuck am I talking about? You're leaving. I was going to ask you if you want to come and watch Roma at my place. They're playing Turin. I completely forgot you're leaving. And we'll see you at Cristiano's fiftieth."

"Lello old fellow, I've told Mom, everyone. I'll come more often. I promise."

He nods, although he is still despondent about his friend leaving.

The line is slow. The air fills with an unmistakable fragrance. Marcello inhales deeply.

"Someone has started celebrating. Do you remember when we used to get stoned too?"

"Of course I remember. How long did that last?"

"A couple of years. In that respect we were lucky compared to so many people who ruined their lives. You were uptight about it; you said you couldn't draw how you wanted. Vanessa found it disgusting. Cristiano thought it was a waste of money, like everything else. Francesco was an athlete. I got high again a couple of years ago. You know those salamanders hanging from the ceiling?"

Gabriele started to laugh, nodding.

"Imagine a five foot three, one hundred and ninety pound salamander hanging from the ceiling with the giant eyes they have. I had a memorable panic attack. Never again. How about you in Milan?"

Gabriele cannot respond; he has doubled over with laughter at the image of Lello the salamander. It takes him a while to recover.

"In Milan, none that I know of, at least among the people I hang out with. They're almost all vegans; they're careful about everything."

Their turn has finally come.

They enter.

The smell.

Of past life and mold, of tobacco that has penetrated everywhere and of air fresheners, the kind that try to hide the stench of stuffiness and end up becoming a foul odor themselves, only more cloying.

Smell kindles memory like no other sense.

For an indefinite length of time, Gabriele does not know the day, month or year of his life.

He is suspended, encapsulated within a timeless time.

His mind cannot even tell itself how wonderful this feeling is.

And it is already over.

7

The cloakroom is empty.

Gone are the counter and the closets where clothes were hung.

Now it is a compartment with moldy walls next to the curtains that serve as the entrance to the actual venue.

"I'll write to Camilla for a second. There might not be signal inside."

Marcello nods, staying by Gabriele's side. They stand slightly to one side to let other guests pass.

Hi Chamomile, I'm entering the party.

She is online.

She writes back. Have fun for me, too. Lots of kisses.

"Aren't you Gabriele, Mauro the Fish's son? The one who made millions from furniture?"

A big, tall man, his pockmarked face covered with a beard, hugs him.

"It's been a while! You've made a bundle, lucky you."

"It's Gianfranco, Leone, the one who was in middle school with us."

Marcello, with his discretion and build, would make a perfect prompter.

"Hi Gianfranco, great to see you. Are you doing okay?"

"Pretty good. I had a little addiction problem. I did a couple of stupid things, and I did some time in jail. But I'm clean now. We've all got some skeletons in our closet, after all. You, too. To get where you are, you had to fuck that old guy in the photo, right? That's life."

What upsets Gabriele, what leaves him feeling powerless, is that for this total stranger before him—with whom he spent a few school years of his childhood—that damned photo raises no doubts but only certainties. And these certainties—looking at his face, a face that is hideous by nature and consumed by the life he has led—need no further comment. A fact like any other, without even the need for a platitude, an adjective.

This is how life works.

He feels himself sinking.

There will always be someone who, on the basis of that photo, can curse life and all those like Gabriele, those who accepted any compromise in order to make it.

"Gianfranco, you didn't have a little addiction problem. You snorted the whole of Venezuela. And sure enough you're burned out, wrecked. You haven't just messed with your brain; your sight is ruined too. In the photo, Gabriele isn't kissing the old guy; you can see from a mile away that it's an optical effect, that there's half a yard between them. But you need to take a good look at it and in your condition that's impossible. Gabriele has always been amazing at drawing, like you are at stealing things from apartments."

Marcello fearlessly confronted their former schoolmate, who is about twelve inches taller than him. But now, after the adrenaline rush, his courage slowly gives way in the face of Gianfranco's bearded, pockmarked face, which has become a mask of hatred.

"Damned dwarf. You should thank God we're at Cristiano's party, or I'd kill you with one touch and this time I'd come out of jail in a wooden suit. Just remember one thing: if you see me, even from a distance, cross the street, beat it. Damned dwarf. Understood?"

Marcello stands frozen on the spot, terrified as anyone would be when faced with an animal-man possessed by rage that threatens to turn into violence.

Gianfranco slides past.

Gabriele gets his breath back.

"Lello old fellow, are you crazy? You shouldn't have gotten involved. You live here. What will happen now?"

He instantly straightens up and regains his smile.

"What will happen how, Gabriele? Nothing. I almost died, but it's over now. Now he'll go inside, drink two gallons of Negroni, and go to the bathroom to snort five or six grams of coke. When he sees me tomorrow, he won't even remember. Sure as day. Don't worry."

They exchange glances. Perhaps because of the averted danger or the absurdity of the whole situation, they start laughing uncontrollably. Thanks to Marcello, Gabriele has rediscovered the immense gift of teary-eyed laughter.

"Lello, you have to stick by me tonight. If someone lays into me about that photo again, I don't want to react the wrong way. And I know that I won't remember a lot of the people I meet."

"You don't have to ask me, I would've stuck by you anyway."

8

The red, heavy velvet curtain, once drawn, makes the light explode in the guests' eyes.

The large room is brightly lit.

And it has remained as it was.

"So! Since he's like a brother and if I don't tell you, you'll all start busting his balls, I can confirm: yes. The guy who came in with Lello is Gabriele Bilancini. Like all true friends, even though he's made money and he lives in Milan, he's here celebrating with me and the rest of you."

Cristiano spoke with a microphone; the effect he created was the exact opposite of what he—in good faith—had in mind.

Everyone looks at Gabriele, and everyone approaches him one step at a time.

He turns white and clings to Marcello; by contrast, his friend smiles at him, telling him with his eyes that he is there for him and he should take it easy.

Fortunately, no one seems hostile; the opposite, if anything.

Gabriele simply repeats "hi" to everyone who comes to shake his hand or hug him. Occasionally, for a bit of variety, he throws in a few "thanks."

The amount of selfies and smiles he is forced to dish out is what he struggles with most, but it could be worse, and he knows it.

At least the little crowd saves him from having to remember names and faces.

It is the turn of a guy a little older than him; unlike the others, he has a melancholic look.

"Do you remember me?"

"I could never forget you. Not in a thousand lifetimes. Hi Domenico, it's so great to see you again."

The embrace between the two is serious, different from the others.

"I can't forget your sister."

"Alessia, Little Alessia. It's been twenty-five years, a quarter of a century, Gabriele. You were both so beautiful, so small. She stayed small forever."

"Certain diseases shouldn't exist, at least for children."

"And yet they do. But I don't want to spoil your evening. Have a great time and congratulations on everything you've done. I think my sister gave you a hand from where she is now."

Gabriele's lip quivers.

"Yes."

"Excuse me for a second, I'm the birthday boy."

Already on a high, wearing a slightly shiny black suit, his tie no more than two fingers wide, Cristiano is approaching again.

"This is my wife."

"Gabriele. Nice to meet you."

"Roberta. Likewise. I wanted to congratulate you."

"Only your husband deserves congratulations tonight. Look at him. He's forty years old and he looks like a little boy."

On hearing these words he smiles, displaying all of his limited charm.

Roberta is a simple girl, wearing a red dress that is not very flattering to her figure.

"No wonder, he still leads a child's life. He works of course, but in the afternoons, woe betide anyone who touches Via Lemonia and his lifelong friends. It's like he has a double job. But that's okay. I'm used to it now."

"That's right, my love."

Cristiano gives her a kiss and she accepts it. Now it is the feeling of bitterness that prevails in her eyes; she does not really seem accustomed to the life that has befallen her. Let alone happy.

"Come here, let me give you a hug, buddy."

Gabriele lets the birthday boy embrace him, then it is Marcello's turn.

"Lello old fellow, I really love you. You've been the heart and soul of the group. Without you, we wouldn't have been friends, right Gabriele?"

"That's true, yeah. He always came to scold us when we were fighting or hanging out with other people."

"What can I say, I'm an only child. I found you and never left you."

Cristiano pulls Gabriele back into the embrace; now the three of them are hugging.

Then he breaks away and turns the microphone back on.

"Now that we're all here, I'll tell you the program for the evening. On the other side of the room, as you can see, they have just finished setting up the buffet, accompanied by wine and prosecco. For cocktails you have to ask at the bar; they're free too of course."

"HAPPY BIRTHDAY CRISTIANO! GIVE IT UP FOR HIM!!!"

A shout starts from nowhere.

The applause is general and very long.

Cristiano is moved; he makes a kind of bow.

"Thank you, thank you all for being here tonight. But most of all for having shared an important part of life together. Now let's all go eat!"

9

The background music is a mix of hits starting from the late ’90s until around the end of the next decade. It opened with Jovanotti’s *L’ombelico del mondo* followed by Christina Aguilera’s *Beautiful*. Now Coldplay’s *Viva La Vida* is playing.

Gabriele is drinking prosecco.

It does not look like his first glass.

Someone covers his eyes from behind.

He feels their hands to see who it is.

He smiles.

“Vanessa.”

“That was easy.”

“True. As soon as I felt your long nails, I told myself: it’s her. You look great.”

She is wearing a long, tight-fitting dress that shows off her figure paired with very high heels.

“Thanks sweetie. I was late because I had to fill in for a colleague who was off sick. I had to work on the cash register until nine o’clock. Such a pain in the ass.”

Vanessa speaks to Gabriele in a different way. After this morning’s chat, it is as if she has laid down her weapons. Now that she is natural, less concerned about making a good impression, she seems like a different girl, more likeable and cheerful.

“And how do I look?”

Francesco appears. He tries to give his fullest smile.

“Great. Francesco, you look great.”

"It's true. You've got a nice complexion. But mind you don't drink too much, since with meds . . . "

It is Marcello who spoke, the one with the lowest alcohol tolerance; in fact, he is already slurring his speech.

"Lello old fellow, you're the drunkest guy here and remember that you're on psychiatric drugs too."

Vanessa gives him a motherly caress.

Meanwhile, the buffet has been demolished.

There is almost nothing left on the trays or inside the heated pans where the starters were arranged.

The two young waiters, aged no more than twenty, stood out at the opening of the buffet with their spruced-up appearance, straight backs and perfectly styled hair. Now it looks like they have run a half marathon in a black suit and white shirt.

"There's some fabulous seafood linguine. If there's any left, I'll go get some for you," Marcello offers Vanessa. She shakes her head.

"Thanks, Lello. I had dinner at home. I knew the buffet would be over by the time I got here, so I ate earlier."

Gabriele has eaten a couple of tea sandwiches; now he opts for a slice of lukewarm pie with an unspecified vegetable filling.

"HAPPY BIRTHDAY CRISTIANO!"

Another round of applause and another glass emptied down everyone's throat.

Still armed with the microphone, Cristiano performs a new bow that is even less harmonious and successful than the first; alcohol is putting his balance to the test.

"Thank you, my darlings. So, this is the plan. Now we've got the cake. Then, before we all start dancing, there's a surprise. But let's take it one step at a time."

Out of what used to be the adults' room—now a huge empty space where only the open security door has survived—comes a huge three-tiered cake. With forty candles and an endless array of sparklers.

Gabriele is still staring at the large room they could once only imagine.

"Do you remember how many times we tried to peek in there?"

Marcello looks at him with his inebriated eyes.

"You won't believe it, Gabriele, but I was thinking the exact same thing."

They have no time to say anything else to each other as the inevitable tune—like a stadium chorus—has now commenced:

"HAPPY BIRTHDAY TO YOU, HAPPY BIRTHDAY TO YOU, HAPPY BIRTHDAY CRISTIANO, HAPPY BIRTHDAY TO YOU!"

Yet another round of applause.

He embraces his wife.

This is unquestionably the best moment of his life.

10

The huge cake has been cut into pieces.

The two waiters, trotting around the room, are serving portions to the many guests. Now their appearance just looks endearing.

Meanwhile, still at a low volume, Mika's *Grace Kelly* plays from the speakers.

"I don't like these sponge cakes."

Marcello does not approve; along with Francesco, Gabriele and Vanessa, he has sat down on one of the many faded red sofas arranged on either side of the room.

"What's the time?"

Marcello is the one to ask.

"Eleven fifteen."

"How? Impossible."

Francesco answered him looking at his phone.

"Lello, it's obvious that your perception of time is messed up. You've been eating and drinking for almost two hours non-stop. I counted six plates full of everything, then I got tired of counting."

"It's nervous hunger."

"Sure. And my name is Cristiano Ronaldo. Did you have nervous hunger as a kid too? You've always eaten for five."

"Lello old fellow, Francesco is right. Now it's all from nerves, but you've always had a ravenous appetite."

"Actually, I don't think my doctor has really figured it out."

Gabriele, Francesco and Vanessa start laughing; as usual, Marcello follows suit.

"Everything is okay, right?"

It is Cristiano. He has approached their couch, drenched in sweat, also visibly affected by the many toasts.

"I'm going around saying hi to everyone, so I don't risk upsetting anyone. I'll come and sit with you here in a moment."

He blows a kiss and darts off.

He looks just like a groom and the evening resembles a proper wedding. The anomaly is the limited presence, or rather the absence, of the bride.

Roberta, Cristiano's wife, sat down as soon as she entered and stayed there. She is surrounded by a rather elderly man and woman, perhaps her parents, as well as a handful of teenagers and a couple of children.

Throughout the evening, while other guests talked and moved around the room, they stood there still and serious, like a tribe invited by strangers to a ceremony that is not theirs.

Gabriele stares at her.

He has tremendous respect for that girl.

He thinks highly of her.

Without knowing her.

She does nothing to hide her unhappiness.

Let alone to disguise the distance between her and everyone else invited to her husband's birthday.

She is fiercely aloof.

She shows it, and she is well aware of it.

She does not imitate, she does not act, she does not condescend.

He would go and talk to her if he had more confidence, but it does not really feel appropriate, and anyway what would he tell her? "I envy you because you have the courage that I lack."

He is distracted by a movement.

Next to the bar, in front of one of the club's black walls, they are setting something up. It is clear now: the two waiters have opened a portable projection screen; they secure it tightly on its tripod.

Cristiano stands in the center of the room, holding the microphone that he now uses with the confidence of a professional presenter.

"It took us a long time, almost a year, to prepare this surprise. This is a gift for all of us, especially my lifelong friends. I don't have to name names because you know who they are."

All eyes are on Marcello, Francesco, Vanessa and Gabriele.

"Just one more thing: get your handkerchiefs ready."

As soon as he finishes speaking, the hoarse, unmistakable voice of Louis Armstrong starts playing loudly.

What a Wonderful World.

The room lights dim.

11

The white screen comes to life.

Yellowed, ravaged by time, photographs begin to appear, moments from the lives of those in the room.

The first sends a shiver down everyone's spines.

Tina, Marcello's mother, holds hands in front of San Policarpo Church with a child who is identical to her child today. Tina, the bed-shaped woman, standing and smiling.

Then comes a gruff-looking man, smoking a cigarette at a table outside Signor Antonio's bar. You only have to take a good look at him: Cristiano's father; he has the same unrelenting eyes. Dead for years.

And Signor Antonio himself, all wrapped in yellow and red for Roma's Italian championship victory in 2001. Via Lemonia can be seen in the background, full of people mad with joy.

A little girl as beautiful as the sun smiling for the camera. A barely twelve-year-old Vanessa.

Her again in the next shot, only older, fifteen years old, holding hands with a similarly aged Gabriele with no beard and short hair.

As more photos scroll by, there is a continuous murmur in the room: everyone who sees themselves captured is overcome with amazement, joy, and nostalgia.

Marcello, ever since he saw his mother, has been shamelessly sobbing along with Vanessa and many others who are rediscovering past loves that are no longer present.

The departed. Gone.

The photograph that now fills the darkened room pierces Gabriele.

Him as a little boy, no more than eight years old, smiling; just behind, leaning against the pillar of his workshop, his father, arms folded, younger, long-haired, looking at his son like a guardian angel.

And Francesco, proudly smiling in a Milan jersey, telling the world with his expression: "Look at me."

Roberta appears too. She hugs Cristiano with a smile that so far no one has seen since.

Armstrong's voice fades out.

Then, like the final burst of a fireworks display, an even older photo. It must be from the early '80s. Five girls embracing on the low wall that still divides Via Lemonia from the park, even though at the time it was just an expanse of garbage and little else.

"No."

The timing with which the denial, of sheer disbelief, comes out of the mouths of Gabriele, Vanessa, Francesco and Marcello is almost frightening; their cheeks are all streaked with tears. Cristiano looks at them with a smile full of love.

Tania, looking stunning, and Tina, together with Gabriella, Cristiano's mother, Vanessa's mother, Luisa, and finally Paola, Francesco's mother.

Five girls embracing, unaware of life, of the fate that lay ahead of each of them, friend or foe, benign or malign.

What a Wonderful World comes to an end.

Endless applause erupts.

"THANKS CRISTIANO, YOU'RE THE MAN!"

The shouts that follow all resound with the same gratitude.

Many guests are drying their eyes.

The light comes on.

Cristiano tries to speak into the microphone but is forced to immediately turn it off. The wave of emotions has provoked a fit of weeping that he cannot quell. Perhaps he had not foreseen it himself.

He makes a superhuman effort to recover, keeping his eyes closed for a few seconds. When he reopens them, he is able to smile.

Here he is again in the guise of the evening's presenter.

"I told you to get your handkerchiefs ready."

"I LOVE YOU, CRISTIANO!" someone shouts from the back of the room.

"I love you too. But I can't see from this distance, and I don't know who you are. But you can count on this: I love everyone in here."

Endless applause breaks out.

Gabriele is overwhelmed, carried away by feelings.

"And now my darlings, after the tears it's time to dance. EVERYONE ON THE DANCE FLOOR!"

Before Cristiano has time to finish speaking, *Seven Nation Army* by the White Stripes blasts from the speakers, this time at very high volume; the lights go out again, and in their place colored spotlights and a strobe light explode in the darkness, bringing the dance floor to life.

Many of the guests get up from the sofas to dance.

Vanessa stands up first and reaches out her arms toward her friends, all of whom stand up to hit the dance floor. With great effort, given their now obvious intoxication.

Gabriele looks at the time on his phone: it is quarter past midnight.

"I have to go."

He tries to tell his friends, but the music is so loud that no one can hear him. He grabs Marcello, then Francesco, who in turn blocks Vanessa.

With gestures, Gabriele signals to his friends that it is time for him to leave.

"JUST ONE DANCE!" Vanessa shouts in his ear.

But he points to the time on his phone: it is getting late.

Cristiano arrives at the same time and sees their exchange but cannot understand. It is Marcello, through gestures, who explains what is going on.

Cristiano, holding up his index finger, tries to repeat Vanessa's invitation: at least one dance together.

Gabriele regretfully shakes his head. "It's too late." They can read his lips.

Marcello waves everyone out of the room for a moment.

Talking and saying goodbye to each other would be impossible in there.

VI
Anio Novus Aqueduct

1

The group gathers outside.

"You could've at least had one dance with us!"

Marcello returns to the charge. He is struggling to stand now, swaying.

"Lello old fellow, I'm wrecked like you. And you've forgotten that I've never danced in my life."

"It's true. Now that you mention it, we had so many fights because I wanted to go clubbing and you didn't!"

Vanessa remembered.

"Exactly. Besides, I have an early train tomorrow morning, so I'd like to have breakfast with Mom and Dad, and spend some time with them before I leave."

There is an awkward silence. Francesco gets the first cold shiver.

"It's fine during the day, but it's still cold at night."

It is Vanessa's turn.

"Yeah."

Everyone looks at Gabriele, and Gabriele looks back at them.

"I told my mom and dad, my sister, and all of you too. It won't be another eight years. Next time I'll come down with Camilla too. She has been asking me for ages."

Sweaty, hot, and drunk, no one responds. Silence prevails again.

Cristiano smiles, hugs Gabriele and holds him close for a few moments.

Then he lets him go.

"You know my name. Cristiano Pontrelli. Sincere to the point of being an asshole. I don't know if you'll come back more often. I honestly don't think so, but it doesn't matter. Let's forget about the future tonight. You were here today. The happiness you've given me by being here with us is inside me, and no one can take it away. As for the rest, what will be, will be."

Gabriele grabs Cristiano back, clutching him because of what he said, the way he looked at him.

"Thanks. Thank you all. I don't deserve friends like you. I'm a guy who doesn't deserve shit."

"What the fuck are you talking about? You're Gabriele Bilancini, the friend everyone wishes they had."

Marcello shouted this, momentarily clinging to Gabriele's back; he looks toward Vanessa and Francesco.

The five of them come together in one big embrace.

They weep because life makes you weep when pain flares up, or when love, as at this moment, overflows from the body.

"You're pretty wasted. Are you sure you don't want someone to keep you company?"

Marcello makes this suggestion to Gabriele, who gives him a caress.

They used to say it to each other all the time when he was a kid, after he had gotten into some trouble or had a fight and made up: Lello rhymes with *fratello*, 'brother'.

"Don't worry about it. You're in a worse state than me. If you come with me, who'll bring you back here? All of you go back inside. You'll catch pneumonia out here."

A kiss for Francesco.

"Take care, Francesco. I'm sure the worst period will pass."

He nods. As always, he is the first not to believe it but does all he can to make everyone else think otherwise.

It is Vanessa's turn. Another kiss, hands clasping.

"I wish you everything you deserve, Vanessa, with all my heart."

She also nods; unlike Francesco, however, she wants to believe it, she has to believe it.

The final glances.

"Bye, then."

Now Gabriele is on one side.

His friends are on the other.

2

He is staggering. Not just his body.

Gabriele is a wandering castaway.

Alcohol mixes feelings like colors on a palette, just for the fun of mixing them, the way a child would.

He could not say how he feels or name the pain that is actually the sum total of everything that is passing through him.

Perhaps a name does not even exist.

Perhaps he is inventing this tremendous pain right now.

Yes.

No one has experienced it before.

He looks up at the stars and feels an urge to ask for help.

Unwittingly, gazing up at the sky, he does not notice a hole in the sidewalk.

He falls flat on his face.

He gets up, stunned, checks his hands, and touches his knees.

No big deal.

The sort of fall that happens to a kid, or a drunk.

The kind that just leaves a few scratches.

He sits for a moment on the low wall that divides the road from Parco degli Acquedotti.

The moon shines three-quarters full.

His eyes sweep along the black expanse of countryside, topped by the rows of giants placed there an eternity ago.

Elephants which, as a child, he imagined returning to their home at night.

Gabriele stares at them, his mouth hanging open, his gaze refusing to believe what he is seeing.

The aqueducts, the elephants, are leaving.

Gabriele is terrified. He puts his hands over his eyes; he wants to remove them from his face. When he reopens them, everything is the same, down to the last detail.

They are silently heading toward the horizon.

"Not you."

Gabriele rises to his feet, staggers monstrously, jumps the wall on which he was sitting and starts running toward the brick beasts that have set off on their way.

Gabriele runs in the park, in the darkness. He falls and gets up, then falls again.

He reaches one of the aqueducts.

It is all true.

Without dignifying him with a glance, a gesture of attention, those giants keep moving in a line, a herd that does not breathe or make a sound.

"Don't go!"

He implores them, but they pay no attention.

"Please! Don't go!"

Those animals do not seem to have ears.

Gabriele cries out again, holding his head in his hands.

"Please, don't go! What can I do without you? I need you!"

The herd does not listen to the human.

"NO! You have to stay here! HERE!"

Gabriele grasps the brick paw of one of the animals in the line; it is so huge and powerful that it lifts him with its step, but Gabriele does not let go.

"Then I'll go where you're going! But I won't leave you!"

Again, as the behemoth that he is clinging to takes a step, it lifts him off the ground like a blade of grass.

"Go, go, but I won't leave you!"

Slowly, clutching the aqueduct, Gabriele goes from despair to sleep, or rather, to blackout.

He stays like this with his eyes closed.

3

Tania opens her eyes.

She picks up her phone charging on the bedside table beside her: it is four in the morning.

Trying not to make the slightest noise, as usual, she gets up.

She goes to the bathroom.

Then to the kitchen, taking a sip of water directly from a bottle.

She is about to return to bed, but a thought holds her back.

She walks on tiptoes to Gabriele's room.

She slowly opens the door.

Tania's smile defeats the darkness.

She goes back to bed.

Still in a state of grace.

She cannot resist sharing it.

She takes one of her husband's hands and shakes it.

"Mauro?"

It takes him a while to wake up and regain a little clarity.

"Everything okay?"

"More than okay. Brilliant. You know how Gabriele didn't want to go to Cristiano's party?"

"Well?"

"It's four and he still hasn't come back. I knew it. You can never forget your friends, the neighborhood where you grew up."

"I'm glad. I'm going back to sleep."

Tania remains staring at the ceiling.

She never needed to be present to live in her son's shoes.

She imagines him with the others, dancing in exhilaration, perhaps thinking about the penthouse she showed him.

She usually cannot fall back to sleep.

Tonight, she can.

Acknowledgements

To wretches who become maestros.
To those who wanted to break their pain with mine.
To everyone who knows how to love much better than I do.

About the Author

Daniele Mencarelli is a poet and author. Born in Rome in 1974, he now lives in Ariccia, Italy. He is a regular contributor to several Italian newspapers and magazines. *Everything Calls for Salvation*, his second novel, won the 2020 Youth Strega Prize. *The House of Gazes*, his first novel, won numerous awards, including the John Fante First Novel Prize and the Volponi Prize.